Ukachi Uwadinobi

Love in the Heat of War

BENANDOR Books—Bronx, NY
ISBN: 979-8-9901271-0-4
eBook ISBN: 979-8-9901271-1-1
Library of Congress Control Number: 2024903670
Title: *Love in the Heat of War*
Author: Ukachi Uwadinobi
Digital distribution | 2024
Paperback | 2024

This is a work of fiction. The characters, names, incidents, places, and dialogue are products of the author's imagination, and are not to be construed as real.

Dedication

To my lovely parents, late Benjamin and Dorcas. My sons, Andy (of blessed memory) and Benjamin. And to my wife, Joy Ini Ubong. Thoughts about them not only supplied me with mental fuel that powered my passion and kept me company during prolonged hours of solitude in my study while writing this novel, but also strengthened my commitment with a sense of purpose that drove it through to fruition.

Other works by Ukachi Uwadinobi
in the pipeline—

Mama What Are You Doing Here?
America Here I Come: A Memoir

Chapter 1

13th August, 1968

BIAFRA ARMY PRIVATE (Pvt.) Udochukwu Abara's heart sank to his stomach, as he panicked and fell backwards, when the enemy Nigerian soldier suddenly jumped out from the rear of an abandoned house and cornered him from behind. The Nigerian soldier aimed the muzzle of his gun at the back of his head at point-blank range, and ordered him to drop his rifle and turn around. He dropped his rifle and instinctively raised his hands in a military sign of surrender. "So this is how I'm going to die, my God!" he pondered feverishly staring into the barrel of his captor's gun. The grim scenario triggered a frisson of terror down his spine. His captor, a burly man in army camouflage with a steel helmet partially covering his eyebrows, spoke with a heavy Yoruba accent, the vernacular of the indigenous tribe of south west Nigeria, when he barked out: "If you move, I will blow your brains out!" The young Biafran soldier, unfamiliar with the rural terrain in Abak, had strayed from the rest of his platoon, when they came under heavy attack by enemy Nigerian forces commanded by Brigadier Taiwo Bamidele. The ferocious surprise attack as dawn was breaking on a Saturday morning, came one month after Biafran troops had launched a counter offensive led by the Biafra Army Special Task Force (STF) to retake Ikot Ekpene. They'd managed to push back the enemy forces and held the ground at Abak frontline.

With no kinetic activity seen at the frontline in the last several weeks, emotional exhaustion had given way to a jolly mood among most of the Biafran soldiers, who were starting to feel sanguine about the war possibly ending soon. Captain Obioma Okoro, 24, Company Commander in the Biafra Army 33 Infantry Battalion at the Abak frontline thought, too that the calm atmosphere was a sign that the war was in its final throes. So he decided to invite Akudo Uwalaka, 20, his fiancée to spend some time with him at Abak, ostensibly convinced there was no longer a looming threat of hostility at the war front that would put her life in peril during her visit. A native of Amawom village, in Oboro-Ikwuano, Umuahia, Eastern Region of Nigeria, Akudo was in Form 3 at Oboro Methodist Grammar School (OMEGRAMS), a mission high school nestled between Umugbalu and Ndoro villages along the Umuahia - Ikot Ekpene road, when the outbreak of war forced the closure of all schools in the Eastern Region of the country. Capt. Okoro, from the neighboring village of Umudike and a product of Government College, Umuahia, was an undergraduate student at the University of Nigeria, Nsukka majoring in Architecture prior to the war. They were dating and looking forward to getting married after Okoro's graduation from Nsukka. Despite his enlistment in the Biafra Army Officers Corps and subsequent deployment to war, starting at the rank of 2nd Lieutenant, their love relationship did not wane. They kept in touch by mail. Akudo, the only daughter of Amos and Rebecca Uwalaka in their late fifties, was determined to go visit Capt. Okoro at the war front against the objection of her parents. They'd tried to talk sense into her, stressing the implicit danger in taking such a trip to the war front but to no avail. Even some close relatives and family friends of the distraught parents, also intervened. Akudo's maternal uncle was strident in his opinion on how to deal with the issue. He urged an aggressive approach the evening he met with Akudo's parents in his house at Amaya compound in Amawom.

"You see, our people say in a proverb that 'You do not stay in a river and allow soap to get into your eyes and cause you to have a burning sensation,'" he said, directing his gaze at Akudo's mother. *"I was so miffed the other day when I overheard someone telling you that your daughter is a grown up, you should let her do whatever she decided to do in this matter. I thought what the fellow was saying to you was piffle, especially not knowing what you're going through with Akudo regarding the potential risk to her life. It is said that 'only the wearer knows where the shoe pinches.' You see me, I have no patience for fey talk. You and your husband seem to be treating your daughter with kid gloves,"* he remarked. *"I know she's your only daughter and everything; but for heaven's sake, she's not a child anymore to be thinking like that and putting you through unnecessary stress. Let's be real for a moment.... This is an issue of life and death, latent with grave consequences. You must not condone an irrational decision. You have to take an aggressive stance and*

stop the nonsense, and not treat your daughter as if she's inviolable. She's a grown woman alright, but if she persists in being irrational, you draw the line on the sand and let her know who the parent is and who the child is! That's all I have to say."

The elderly parents of Capt. Okoro — Pa Okoro Analaba and Ma Agnes Analaba — were equally perplexed and sympathized with Akudo's parents over their emotional ordeal, and did what they could to help. In a letter Pa Analaba sent to his son, Capt. Okoro, he wrote—

My dear son. Greetings to you from your mom and me. How are you and your men doing? We hope you all are doing the best you can to cope under the prevailing circumstance. We continue to pray for God's protection over you and your men. You see, my son, ... the reason I'm writing this letter is to let you know how we feel about the idea you'd proposed to have Akudo, our future daughter-in-law, God willing, go visit with you there at the war front. It is dangerous for her to do so and we don't think it's a good idea. God forbid if something bad happened to her during her visit, you, including your mom and me, would be blamed for it. Mouths would be wagging in the village, and our family would become the subject of scandal. So we are seriously urging you to reconsider your decision and cancel the proposed visit at this time and let us see how things go with this war. For quite some time now, there had been no air raid sirens heard, something that struck me as odd. Perhaps it's an indication of some good news coming soon. I have the belief that by the grace of God, the war will soon end and you come back home to the land of Umudike in one piece, and by then you and your girl will have all the time in the world to live out your dreams together. God bless and continue to protect you and your men.

Your father,
Pa Analaba

The letter purposely written to stop Capt. Okoro and Akudo from following through with their plan did not yield the desired result. As a last ditch effort to derail the planned visit, Akudo's mom turned to her daughter's best friend and high school classmate at Oboro Methodist Grammar School (OMEGRAMS), Comfort Uche, 20, from Ndoro village for assistance. Comfort came over and met with Akudo in her parent's house at Mbakamanu compound, Amawom, to talk one-on-one about the issue of her proposed visit to the war front. They talked for almost an hour. Akudo seemed like she was beginning to lean toward changing her mind, but at the end of the conversation remained adamant.

"*Listen, girl! I know you have the niggling thought that I am right in making the case against your taking this potentially risky trip to the war front, but you're just not willing to admit it,*" said Comfort. "*You're in love with Capt. Obioma Okoro and you're missing him very much. OK, I get it! But you don't seem to appreciate the fact that we're still in a war,*" she stressed, in an attempt to nudge her friend back to reality and quit being irrational and insensitive to the feelings of her parents about the issue. "This is insane acting like that and being oblivious to your parents' feelings and concerns." Despite her best efforts, Comfort, too was unsuccessful in her intervention. Akudo's parents seemed to have exhausted all their options. Other than physically restraining their recalcitrant daughter, they didn't know what else to do to stop her from going. They still couldn't believe her total lack of empathy in light of the depression her irrational decision was causing them. Hell bent on going, off she went, on a busy market day: The popular *Ndoro Market*.

AROUND 7:00 AM ON A FRIDAY, the Umuahia-Ikot Ekpene road saw people, mostly women, carrying their goods on their heads walking towards Ndoro. Noticeably absent were young adult males between the ages of 18 and 40. Most young men of that age group were rarely seen in public during the war because of fear of conscription. Biafra Army personnel often raided the villages to conscript adult males into the army. Akudo had packed her personal belongings in a small suitcase, and had a plastic bag in which she put some food items — gari, dried fish, crayfish, ukazi leaves, ground egusi, ukpo, salt and pepper that she'd bought from Mbaru, Amawom evening market the locals called *'Ahia 4'* (4 P.M. Market) — all wrapped in old sheets of newspaper the day before. There was an awkward moment of uneasiness, when Akudo had grabbed her suitcase and the plastic bag, and muffled under her breath as she walked toward the front door: *"Okay, I'm leaving now, bye."*

Her parents, grim-faced, struggled with the thought

of saying goodbye.

"Okay o," said her dad, as he stared pensively at the door. Her mom, tears trickling down her face, stood by the door with her hands plaintively clutched over her head, watching as she left.

THE MORNING SUN was just beginning to penetrate the clouds, and the road swarming with pedestrian traffic heading toward Ndoro market, provided a subtle cover for Akudo to blend in, without worrying about any unsuspecting relative or friend coming up to ask her where she was traveling to. People would perfunctorily think she was going to Ndoro market, she thought. Public transportation was scarcely available as a result of the war. The situation was exacerbated by the severe economic blockade the federal military government of Nigeria under General Yakubu Gowon had weaponized to cripple the fledgling economy of the nascent Biafra. So Akudo took off on foot and soon was part of the chain of pedestrians heading south toward Ndoro. Traveling during a civil war that had literally decimated the quality of life in the embattled new country — all in the name of love — was a misguided gambit. A trip that ordinarily would take less than an hour in prewar days traveling in a vehicle, took Akudo several hours to get to her destination, riding at times in rickety commercial vehicles few of which were available part of the way, and other times walking the long distance on desolate and treacherous road filled with coarse gravels between Ariam and the neighboring border community of Nto Ndang, until she got to Abak. It would ominously be the last weekend of tranquility in the war torn zone. Regardless of the precarious situation, it was not going to dampen the enthusiasm and expectation the two lovebirds had about the trip — Akudo possibly getting pregnant — during her visit. In a letter she'd written to Capt. Okoro confirming she'd be coming, she'd fantasized about being pregnant with a baby boy and proposed naming the baby: *Obiagha,* which in Igbo means, "Heart of war."

AKUDO ARRIVED THE BIAFRA ARMY 33 INFANTRY BATTALION HEADQUARTERS as the sun was starting to set. Located on a sprawling school premises at the foothills of Obot Akara near a small bridge, it overlooked a swamp with palm wine trees, a major source for top quality locally brewed alcoholic beverage germane to the area. After a young Biafra Army Military Police (MP) with the rank of Corporal at the front gate had briefly questioned Akudo to know who she was and the purpose of her visit, a second MP led the weary looking but attractive, beautiful young lady to the army clerk in a classroom that was turned into a reception area in the Battalion Commander's office. As luck would have it, the army clerk turned out to be someone familiar, who hailed from Amawom, Akudo's village. They exchanged pleasantries. Staff Sergeant Martin Oriaku, the army clerk, used his influence as the administrative assistant to Lieutenant Colonel George Abuajah, Battalion Commander, to get two soldiers as armed military escorts for Akudo. They would lead her to Capt. Okoro's location, three-quarters of a mile from the Abak frontline. It was late in the evening around six-thirty when they arrived. The reception of Akudo in the waiting arms of Capt. Okoro was ecstatic. The highly excited Company Commander grabbed his fiancée and gave her a warm, tight hug. Then holding her by the waist, he lifted her off the ground and dramatically threw her up causing her skirt to flap in the wind, inadvertently exposing her underwear as his soldiers, including the two military escorts gleefully watched. Were it not for the prevailing, inexplicable silence at the frontline in the last several weeks, he'd have ordered his men to fire some rounds of bullets into the sky to simulate the traditional military *'21 - gun salute'* in honor of Akudo marking her safe arrival, he quipped, and locked lips with her in a sultry kiss. After the romantic kiss, the two military escorts stepped backwards, gave Capt. Okoro a military salute, then turned around and headed back to their base at Obot Akara.

Chapter 2

CORPORAL MOSES AKOMA, personal assistant to Capt. Obioma Okoro grabbed Akudo's suitcase and the plastic bag and took them into the house, in front of which only moments ago had been the scene of a heart-warming display of intimate affection by Capt. Okoro and his just-arrived beautiful, young lady visitor. The two lovebirds peered into each other's eyes, smiling as they strolled toward the house, their hands crisscrossed behind each other's back. The rest of Corporal Akoma's peers, who had gleefully watched the dramatic act of romance unfold, like a scene right out of *Romeo and Juliet,* slinked away to their rooms in the compound. The 6-bedroom house with a central quad provided ample accommodation for the troops. Capt. Okoro occupied the master bedroom that was fairly large, and the room adjacent to it served as his office, while the rest of the rooms were used as sleeping areas for his men, with one room for storing their weapons and boxes of ammunition. Surrounded by tall trees with overarching branches of green leaves spanning the rooftop, the environment couldn't be more suitable. Once the two lovebirds got inside the house and were in the master bedroom, Akudo felt at ease and threw herself down on the bed. Capt. Okoro could not contain his excitement and romantic feelings. Akudo was giddy with excitement, too. Okoro began to rummage all over her body until—

"Oh my God, Obim! You are tickling me," Akudo drawled momentarily. "Seriously speaking, you know I'm tired from this tortuous, long trip. You don't know what happened; wait till I tell you the full story. My parents, your parents, even Comfort Uche from Ndoro, you know her, my best friend at Oboro Grammar; my mom had asked her to dissuade me from coming. All of them had strong objections. Darling, the orchestrated efforts they mounted to prevent me from coming almost turned into a small war between me and them. It wasn't easy o."

"Yeah, I know. My father even wrote to me expressing how he and my mother were not pleased about your coming and wanted me to shelve the idea at this time," said Capt. Okoro.

"But we prevailed," said Akudo, adding, "no matter that we're still in a war, I don't care! Nobody can stop us from being together. I've been missing you, Obim."

"I've been missing you much, too," chimed Capt. Okoro, playfully jabbing her in the stomach as he leaned in for a kiss. "Especially since the past several weeks the war front had been relatively quiet. Hard to believe, but it is good for us. In fact, Major General Christian Onwu, our Division Commander, told me last week that military intelligence report from higher-ups at Umuahia, suggested something was in the offing that could see the war come to an end soon."

"Obim, I can't wait to have your baby, honestly! Once the war is over, we can get married. I wouldn't

mind not going back to resume school at OMEGRAMS. I'd rather stay home raising our baby and wait till after you graduate from Nsukka and land a plum job as an architect, then I can go back to OMEGRAMS and finish high school. You saw the name I proposed for the baby in my letter, right? Obiagha!"

Capt. Okoro chuckled and flashed a smile of preening agreement. "Sounds like you read my mind. I was going to tell you that we could get married while you're visiting, so that when the baby arrives, hopefully after the war, won't be out-of-wedlock. I can arrange to have our Army Chaplain, Major Brightson Uwajimgba at Obot Akara perform our marriage ceremony. Would you like that?"

"Of, course! Obim," Akudo enthusiastically affirmed.

Continuing—

"Okay, I know how you feel now, trust me, the feeling is mutual," said Akudo. "But you have to be patient and relax. We have all night. For now, I think I should take a shower and after that, cook egusi soup and make gari we can eat for dinner. I brought some ingredients to make something for you for a change."

Capt. Okoro acquiesced and asked Corporal Moses Akoma, his personal assistant to get water for Akudo to take a shower. Corporal Akoma did as instructed. After Akudo had showered and cooked the egusi soup and made gari, they ate and had a few glasses of drink from a bottle in a case of *Re-Unite* wine Capt. Okoro had saved as a war souvenir. His men had pulled the case of wine among other items from a house Nigerian forces had abandoned as they fled in retreat when

Biafran forces launched a successful counter offensive to retake the area the Nigerian forces had captured and occupied a while back when they first landed. Now relaxed as midnight approached, the two lovebirds were ready to go at it and enjoy a blissful night together.

Chapter 3

SATURDAY MORNING SURPRISE

THE CLOUDS AND MORNING MIST had begun to clear. A phalanx of Nigerian forces had infiltrated the location of the Biafran troops, stealthily cutting them off from behind and unleashed a barrage of gunfire. The whizzing sound of bullets and deafening explosion of landing mortars fired from mobile launchers mounted on Nigeria Army trucks from across the frontline, spelt doom for the Biafran soldiers rattled out of their trenches. In the ensuing disarray, Pvt. Udochukwu Abara and members of his platoon found themselves dislodged and cut-off from behind by the Nigerian forces. It was a clear sign that the past several weeks of eerie silence, had been intentional as a tactical ploy by the Nigerian forces to lull the Biafran troops into thinking that the war was coming to an end. Pvt. Abara raised his hands when he was cornered and captured by the Nigerian soldier who aimed his automatic rifle at him at point blank range and ordered: "If you move I will blow your brains out!"

In the chaos of combat, a few of his platoon members managed to escape through some gaps in the enemy formation, and found their way back to the Biafran side of the frontline. Some others weren't as lucky, they'd been hit by gunfire and died from fatal injuries sustained.

NOT FAR AWAY FROM the main road, where the beleaguered Biafran troops were seen retreating, was the bullet-ridden house Capt. Okoro with Akudo, and his men were occupying. After they'd retired to bed late at night on the heels of Akudo's Friday weekend arrival, the two lovebirds were in the master bedroom enjoying the deep pleasure of intimacy during early morning sex, when suddenly the eruption of gunfire and deafening blasts of mortar shelling from enemy forces, jolted them out of bed. Instinctively Capt. Okoro reached for his automatic rifle he stored under the bed as adrenaline rush kicked in. He turned up the kerosene lamp on the table in the bedroom so he could see. He grabbed his gun, leaned it against the wall and slid into his army uniform.

"Obim! Obim!" Akudo called out apprehensively.

"Are we safe?" her voice quaking, she asked as Capt. Okoro frantically put on his boots with lace untied, grabbed his gun and rustled to the front door. Corporal Moses Akoma, his personal assistant was already on the other side of the door nervously knocking. The rest of the troops had retreated to the rear of the house cowering in fear as the sound of gunfire and exploding mortars intensified. Capt. Okoro pulled back the door. A heart-wrenching wail instantly followed. Like someone having an epileptic fit, Corporal Akoma struggled to get the words out of his mouth.

"Sir! Sir! ...we...we... ha... ha.. have... be... be... been ... sur...sur...rounded by the...enemy soldiers," he stuttered. "I just saw Private Ubochi Oti with a fatal gunshot wound to his right shoulder. He was running towards us from the main road bleeding profusely when he collapsed. Looks like he is dead."

"Sir, the last thing I heard him say before he collapsed was that Lieutenant Pius Atuma and his personal assistant, Pvt. Monday Obiefuna had been killed," said Corporal Akoma, his body shaking, reeling from the shock of exploding artillery shells.

Chapter 4

AKUDO WAS ENGULFED in a frisson of fear that caused her to feel the hair on the back of her head stand.

"Jesus Christ! Is this for real, or a horrible nightmare?" she thought, shivering.

She picked up her wrapper loincloth on the bed and tied it around her waist covering the bottom half of her translucent nightgown and rushed out of the bedroom, braless and without her underwear, her breasts bouncing as she ran toward the door and heard Corporal Moses Akoma sobbing, relaying to Capt. Okoro, the bad news of what had just happened.

"Oh my God!" Akudo exclaimed, stomping her feet and pacing around the room, wailing hysterically. She paused and shook her head. Then gnashed her teeth and uttered in her native Igbo vernacular, "'Chinekem!' (My God!) We are finished…We are finished o!" she wailed in refrain. "Obim, I thought you said everything was fine and assured me we were going to be safe, but now see what is happening."

Completely caught by surprise and addled, Capt. Okoro's mind was torn in different directions. He didn't know what course of action to take. Storm out of the house with his men and open fire without any clear target in his sight? From a tactical military perspective, that idea didn't seem to make sense, he thought. If anything, it would expose him and his men as clear targets and easily mowed down in a volley of gunfire from the enemy forces. It felt like his head was about to explode as the auguries of death rapidly converged in his head. The sad reality of his mortality was unfolding before his very own eyes. Moreover, he felt the overbearing weight of personal liability on his mind concerning the uncertainty of Akudo's safety at that harrowing moment. The smell of gun smoke in the air infiltrated the room and swirled up his nostrils. There was no glimmer of hope left. Everything looked grim. Death, it appeared, was approaching the door, he thought. The Nigerian forces were now advancing from both flanks of the main road toward the house where Capt. Okoro with his men and Akudo were holed up. Then came the order that sent chills down their spines. A Platoon Sergeant of the advancing enemy Nigerian troops stood on the shoulder of the road adjacent to the dirt path leading to the house and darkly announced with a loudspeaker:

"YOU HAVE BEEN SURROUNDED. THERE'S NO WAY FOR YOU TO ESCAPE. YOU ARE NOW ORDERED TO DROP YOUR WEAPONS. REMOVE YOUR CLOTHES, UNIFORM, PANTS, EVERYTHING, AND RAISE YOUR HANDS AND SLOWLY COME OUT ONE BY ONE IN A SINGLE FILE AND WALK TOWARDS THE MAIN ROAD. I REPEAT, REMOVE YOUR CLOTHES, UNIFORM AND RAISE YOUR HANDS, AND SLOWLY WALK OUT IN A SINGLE FILE TOWARDS THE MAIN ROAD WITHOUT YOUR WEAPONS!"

"SIR, WHAT DO WE DO NOW?" asked Corporal

Akoma, struggling to catch his breath.

As tension grew, Akudo, still wailing hysterically, felt they were in dire straits, death staring them in the face. No time for debate on what to do next or brood over their fate that seemed to be getting worse by the minute, she thought. "You are asking your Sir 'what can we do now, hah?' He made me believe that it was safe for me to come visit, and now this…." she sneered at Corporal Akoma, simultaneously taking a swing at Capt. Okoro. Corporal Akoma reflexively thrust his right arm forward to stave off Akudo's hand, but it was too late. Her right palm had viciously landed on Capt. Okoro's face with a bang, Gbam!

"'Chinekem,' (My God), Obim you have killed me! You have killed me o, Obim!" cried Akudo. "I should have listened to my parents who were vehemently against my coming," she railed. "Okay, I'll tell you what I'm going to do now, I'll walk right out of this house!" she declared, dramatically untying her wrapper and taking off her see-through night gown and was naked in front of the embattled Company Commander, who had just taken an unexpected humiliating slap in the face, as his horrified personal assistant, watched. Akudo now completely nude, her eye-popping breasts and the entire anatomy of her femininity in plain view, lurched forward to open the door.

"What are you doing?" Capt. Okoro, dropping his loaded automatic rifle on the floor blurted out in a hushed tone. "Are you out of your mind?" he said, his face contorted with a grimace as he grabbed her wrist to wrest her hand away from the door knob.

"Leave me alone," she protested flailing her arm to

free her wrist from his grip. She succeeded and proceeded to open the door. "In the face of death, what else is there to hide?" she uttered, wryly.

Naked, Akudo stepped out of the house leaving the door partially ajar and walked down the three landing steps to the ground raising her hands above her head. She was now in full view of the enemy Nigerian soldiers who were just a stone's throw away furtively lying in the thick underbrush by the side of the main road with their guns aimed at the house.

Chapter 5

IT WAS ONE THING expecting to see some harried looking Biafran male infantry soldiers emerge from the besieged house in a single file raising their hands above their heads as ordered, and another thing totally the opposite, in the form of a jarring sight of a beautiful, curvy shaped and heavy breasted naked young woman coming out through the front door.

"Oti o! Oti o! Oluwa mi o! (No! No! Oh, my God!),"* blurted out the Nigerian army Sergeant leading the assault team in his native Yoruba vernacular, as Akudo, with her hands raised above her head, slowly advanced toward the main road.

Presuming that Akudo posed no immediate potential threat, the Nigerian army Sergeant made the perilous choice of stepping out of the underbrush to grab her in full view. Capt. Okoro, who thought his life at that point had been absolutely reduced to nothingness, his mind filled with a sludge of humiliation and guilt, thought to himself, "If I'm going to die, I might as well go out in a blaze of glory by taking out at least one or some of these bastards, too."

He lifted his automatic rifle and moved to the left corner of the living room. Looking through a narrow opening in a side window, he had a clear view of the Nigerian Army Platoon leader of the assault team.

The Sergeant, now in the crosshairs of his gun, Capt. Okoro fired his weapon, *krrrah-krrrah-krrrah-krrrah-krrrah!* and continued to shoot, almost emptying the magazine. The bullets broke through the curtain covered glass window and hit the Sergeant near the base of his neck, severing the carotid arteries. He instantly collapsed. Akudo in the path of gunfire narrowly missed being hit. Capt. Okoro and his soldiers hunkered down in the house expecting the worst. The Nigerian Army assault team let loose a volley of gunfire that went on for nearly half an hour. Akudo leapt onto the main road. One of the Nigerian soldiers immediately grabbed her and whisked her to the safety of a waiting Land Rover Jeep military ambulance a short distance away, while other members of the assault team crawled to retrieve the body of their fallen Sergeant, fatally wounded. The combination of rapid gunfire and hand grenades the Nigerian soldiers lobbed into the house set it ablaze. Capt. Okoro and his men had no chance.

The body of the fallen Nigerian Army Sergeant was retrieved and carried on a stretcher to the waiting military ambulance with Akudo sitting in the back compartment, wearing an improvised gown handed to her by one of the Nigerian Army paramedics to cover her body, while the others attended to the casualty. Just before the ambulance was driven off toward a military hospital and detention facility between Abak and Uyo, Akudo saw thick plumes of black smoke rise above the burning house, shooting flames several feet into the air. The acrid smell of human flesh burning, and exploding boxes of ammunition, floated in the air. Silence eerily descended upon the scene.

Akudo broke out crying, "Obim! Obim! Obim... So this is how you have gone and left me. This is how it ended for us."

PUSH BACK

THE SHOCK OF THE WEEKEND ATTACK by the Nigerian forces at the Abak frontline jolted the Biafran troops of the 33 Battalion at Obot Akara into action. Lieutenant Colonel George Abuajah and his top officers mobilized the Battalion soldiers, and called for reinforcement from Umuahia, to repel the advance of the enemy forces from the Ikot Ekpene axis. The stakes were high to keep the Nigerian troops from making further incursion beyond Abak to the rest of the communities along the way to Ikwuano, with the ultimate objective to reach and capture the town of Umuahia, the vestigial stronghold of Biafra. By late evening, reinforcement was on the way.
Mbaru, the local evening market at Amawom village, reverberated with the sound of Biafran martial song....
"We are Biafrans, fighting for our nation; in the name of Jesus, we shall conquer!"
Many people lined both sides of the road, cheering and clapping for the Biafran troops packed in a 10 - truck convoy heading toward Oboro Methodist Grammar School on their way South East to the Ikot Ekpene sector of the war. Suddenly a spontaneous outburst of wailing changed the euphoric mood of the cheering crowd. Someone had spotted a familiar face among the weary looking Biafran troops with a Mark 4 rifle slung over his shoulders, perching precariously

on the tail board of the last truck in the convoy slowly dragging up the hill between Mbaru evening market and Mbakamanu compound in Amawom. It was Chinkwe Agbalanma, a native son of Mbachukwu, Amawom among the Biafran troops spotted in the truck, as he wistfully waved goodbye at onlookers on both sides of the road. Less than 12 hours before, Biafran Army recruiters prowling the villages for able bodied young adult males, had conscripted Chinkwe Agbalanma, 19, during an early morning raid while he was on his way to his family's farm with his elderly parents who watched helplessly as the frightening army recruiters whisked their son away. Young men in the village, evading conscription relied on their women for tip-off whenever army recruiters posing as soldiers on home leave, were suspected to be around. The elders of the village had become wary and cynical of the war propaganda and scared of seeing their young men conscripted and sent off to war, lacking adequate military training and equipment. Chinkwe Agbalanma had been unlucky that morning. It would be the last time he was seen alive.

THE BIAFRAN TROOPS mobilized and sent for reinforcement incredibly put up a tough defense and were not only able to stall the advance of the Nigerian troops but also managed to push them back to the previous frontline at Abak. The push back by the reinforcement troops from Umuahia, in coordination with the men of the 33 Infantry Battalion commanded by Lieutenant Colonel George Abuajah, was at a huge cost. Army doctor Major Joseph (Jack) Umesi, of the Biafra Army Medical Corps, with his team of paramedics, including members of Biafra Red Cross volunteer team from Ikwuano villages, performed valiantly in saving as many lives as they could, in a makeshift medical triage setup at the 33 Battalion HQ at Obot Akara. Among the casualties fatally injured was Pvt. Chinkwe Agbalanma within an hour of getting to the frontline. Staff Sergeant Martin Oriaku, administrative assistant to Lieutenant Col. Abuajah, was the one who sent the message home to the elderly parents of Pvt. Agbalanma at Amawom that their son had been killed. News of his death in the wake of the surprise weekend attack by Nigerian forces at Abak frontline, where Capt. Obioma Okoro was, raised fresh fears in the parents of Akudo Uwalaka. They'd not heard from their daughter for several hours since she left home to go visit her army officer fiancé, Obioma Okoro at the war front. At about 12:00 Noon on Sunday, the next day, air raid sirens went off as villagers ran for cover, when a Nigerian Air Force bomber flew over Amawom toward Umudike Agricultural Institute that was being used for research and development purposes for the Biafra military. The Nigerian Air Force bomber had circled Umudike twice and dropped bombs, one of which had missed the pilot's target and landed in a residential area in Amawom, killing one person and created a huge crater in the ground large enough to contain two Volkswagen Kombi buses. Akudo's parents saw the air raid fatality as an ill omen. They held their breath and feared for the worst, as news spread around the village that the battle at Abak, which took Biafran troops by surprise, had claimed many lives on the Biafran side.

Chapter 6

THE NIGERIAN SOLDIER who captured 20-year-old Biafra Army Pvt. Udochukwu Abara took out a bayonet from a belt pouch worn around his waist and attached it to the muzzle of his gun. The optics of a bayonet sent shivers down the spine of the young Biafran soldier, causing him to scream at the top of his voice, "Mama, mo!" as his captor charged toward him in a manner that ominously suggested the unthinkable was about to happen.

"Please, Sir! Please Sir! I beg you in the name of God, don't kill me, please don't kill me," he frantically begged, groaning with labored respiration.

"Now, move!" ordered the Nigerian soldier.

As they moved, at times stumbling, walking through the bloodstained brush of wild grass, Udochukwu Abara felt pessimistic about his immediate fate. He's being marched to some remote location in the area, where he'd be executed and dumped in a trench and left to rot, he grimly thought. As they marched along, he unavoidably stepped on the bodies of some of his fellow Biafran soldiers hit by enemy bullets, some with gaping wounds in the chest bleeding profusely and moribund. Others with eyes blown out of their sockets, limbs torn apart and fragments of muscle tissues dangling. Seemingly insensitive to the gruesome sight of the fatally wounded Biafran soldiers lying in the puddles of blood, the Nigerian soldier following closely behind Udochukwu Abara, with gun trained at his back, sarcastically remarked: "You see them? That's the prize of war for boys like you brought to the war front to fight."

The trail led them to a dirt road off the main coal tar road overlooking the federal prison at Abak town. A Nigerian Army truck was parked on the shoulder of the road a short distance away. Udochukwu Abara's captor told him to proceed to the waiting truck. When they got to the truck, he noticed about half a dozen captured Biafran soldiers, blindfolded and sitting on their buttocks on the bare floor in the back of the truck. He was ordered to climb inside, and was blindfolded, too. The truck was driven off to a military base situated 10 miles away along the road to Uyo. The captured Biafran soldiers on arrival were separated and taken to different locations at the military facility for detention and interrogation. The army considered them to be military assets as potential sources for military intelligence information to be collected when questioned by Nigerian army military Intelligence officers. Information obtained from captured soldiers would be useful for military purposes at the war front. Part of the initial protocol on arrival at the facility, was conducting physical and mental examination of the captives. A mental assessment by a military psychologist was necessary to determine cognition in the context of the required interrogation to follow. The assessments also included the collection of personal information for records purposes that would be fed into the Nigerian Army database on captured Biafran soldiers held as prisoners of war (POW) at a military prison in Calabar. Udochukwu Abara's personal information, included—

UDOCHUKWU RAYMOND ABARA. HAILS FROM AFARA, IBEKU, UMUAHIA. FORM 3 STUDENT AT ANGLICAN GRAMMAR SCHOOL, IBEKU, UMUAHIA BEFORE THE OUTBREAK OF WAR. ENLISTED RANK IN BIAFRA ARMY: PRIVATE....

The results of physical and mental assessments of Pvt. Udochukwu Abara showed he was physically and mentally fit to undergo the interrogation. During the process, he was asked about the location of Biafran troops in the area where he was captured, who their commanding officers were, the size and strength of their infantry, military assets, etc., all valuable pieces of intelligence information necessary for the Nigerian Army Military Intelligence Unit to assess and determine the enemy troops' capabilities.

"It'll be to your advantage to tell me the truth and nothing but the whole truth while answering the questions I'm going to ask you," said the Nigerian Army Lieutenant military intelligence officer sitting across the table from Udochukwu Abara in the interrogation room.

"Yes, Sir!" he nodded, visibly still trembling.

"Relax," said the interrogating officer. "I know you're traumatized, but don't be afraid. You're not going to be killed, you're lucky you were captured alive without any physical injury sustained, you hear me?"

"Yes, Sir!" said Udochukwu Abara. He needed to hear those words of assurance, like an emotional alchemy at that point. "Thank you Sir! God bless you Sir!"

He would answer the litany of questions directed at him without feeling guilty as a traitor. At that point, he wasn't worrying about thinking of himself as a saboteur giving valuable military information to the enemy. All he cared about was to stay alive. Whatever he could say or do to stay alive was all that mattered. The thoughts of his parents and family members back home in Biafra – like wondering how they were doing, what might be their fate in the days ahead, given the surprise offensive of the Nigerian forces aiming to advance toward what was remaining of Biafra, his hometown of Umuahia – were far removed from his mind. In his responses to the questions asked, he provided answers that were a treasure trove of information in precise details, including the location of the Biafra Army Company and its commanding officer, Capt. Obioma Okoro and his men, viewed as the toughest fighting force of the 33 infantry Battalion at the Ikot Ekpene axis. But unknown to him, Capt. Okoro and his men had perished at the location he'd disclosed and reduced to rubble and ashes in the aftermath of the stealthy weekend attack by enemy Nigerian forces. Udochukwu Abara would subsequently be transferred to a military prison in Calabar as a prisoner of war.

Chapter 7

AKUDO WAS AS DEFIANT and uncooperative with the Nigerian military authorities as she was with her parents back home at Amawom when they were trying everything they could to dissuade her from taking the trip to the war front. While in the military ambulance, wailing hysterically after seeing the thick plumes of black smoke from the house her fiancé, Capt. Okoro — now presumed dead, was occupying with his men less than an hour ago — she made a dramatic scene that the paramedics deemed unacceptable. She was pounding repeatedly on the rear glass window of the ambulance, causing it to break.

"Why don't you people just kill me, after killing my man, and my people?" she railed, trolling the Nigerian military paramedics in the ambulance. "What's the point of bringing me into this ambulance, to watch the dead body of your soldier, hah?"

Out of compassion and courtesy, the Nigerian military paramedics had initially decided not to have Akudo in handcuff, being a woman, who'd also been exposed to the grim spectacle of warfare. But her destructive conduct, which seemed to indicate she was having an acute mental health crisis, necessitated a physical restraint. So she was handcuffed.

Apart from the motionless body of the Sergeant in

the military ambulance, the Nigerian forces had incurred a smaller number of casualties in the Saturday early morning offensive they launched at the Abak frontline than the Biafran forces had sustained. Having misjudged the last several weeks of no kinetic activity, the Biafran forces had relaxed, thinking the war might be over soon. Akudo was driven in the military ambulance with the fallen army Sergeant to the same military facility along Uyo road, where Udochukwu Abara and his fellow captured Biafran soldiers were taken to. The body of the dead soldier was removed and carried on a stretcher to a morgue. Akudo was led to an office to be processed and evaluated. She would be seen by a military intelligence officer for interrogation.

She proved to be a tough case to handle during interrogation. She was defiant, disrespectful and uncooperative with the army military intelligence officer questioning her. It became clear to the officer that she was having a mental meltdown, ostensibly precipitated by the trauma of exposure in a war zone, and thought she needed to see a mental health professional. The military Intel officer then referred her to a military psychologist on the army base. The session with a psychologist subsequently led to her transfer to a military hospital at Oron, where she was briefly under the care of an Egyptian psychiatric doctor. The doctor determined that Akudo was suffering from severe post-traumatic stress disorder related to her war front exposure. She was exhibiting signs and symptoms of auditory and visual hallucinations, which according to the doctor could potentially lead to a more serious mental illness. In the evaluation report, the doctor recommended that she be transferred to a major psychiatric facility far away from the Southeastern Nigeria sector of the war, for a more comprehensive care.

UNEXPECTED NEWS

A NEW DEVELOPMENT in Akudo's physical examination added a critical dimension to the urgency around her care. Akudo reported that she had missed her period. A pregnancy test result was positive. It created a whole new dynamic that accelerated the doctor's referral recommendation for her transfer to a major mental health care facility. Meanwhile, her pregnancy piqued the curiosity of care providers in the military facility at Oron. Ordinarily it wouldn't have mattered that much under normal circumstances. But the circumstance under which she was brought to the facility was not an ordinary normal circumstance. So when care providers had inquired about her pregnancy, ostensibly while under military custody, she was quick to let them have it, without mincing words—

"Since you want to know how my pregnancy came about; .... It was my man, whom your people killed."

"Oh, Miss, I'm sorry to hear this," said the Egyptian psychiatrist, alluding to the circumstance related to her capture as the admission note in her medical record showed.

Few days later, the doctor informed Akudo that arrangements had been made to fly her to Lagos, where she'd receive a more comprehensive care in light of her mental and medical status. The facility in

Lagos ended up being a government run hospital – *Yaba Psychiatric Center.*

Chapter 8
MEETING THE FRENCH LADY

THE MILITARY PRISON COMPLEX in Calabar housed offices used by civilian personnel. Among the civilian personnel working in the prison was a French lady and member of the International Green Cross named Collette Durand. A beautiful blond in her early thirties, soft spoken, caring and compassionate; Ms. Durand was an elementary school teacher in Paris, France when she met her husband, Pierre Richard, a French native and an accountant by profession in December of 1966. They were married not long afterwards.

An unspeakable tragedy struck in June of 1967, when her husband died in a ghastly motor accident in Paris. The young widow, devastated and morbidly depressed, looked for something that would give her a new sense of direction and purpose in life. She joined the French Red Cross. The Nigeria-Biafra war that began in July of 1967 had caught her attention. Over the course of time as the war progressed, her attention was drawn to the plight of soldiers fighting in the war, especially the Biafran soldiers and the hundreds of thousands of civilians suffering from malnutrition, *kwashiorkor,* with children being the most afflicted. Watching on French television news almost every night — the horrific sight of innocent children dying from the brutalities of the war — was heartbreaking. She searched for how she could make a difference and found the French Red Cross to be a good place to start. So she joined the French Red Cross. It paved the way for her recruitment in the International Green Cross in Geneva. Her plan paid off. She became a member of the world acclaimed international agency for humanitarian aid. Her boss, Dr. Alan McCollom, Executive Director for global affairs and assignments, sent her to Nigeria. There, she was sent to a Nigerian military prison in Calabar to monitor how prison custodial staff were treating captured Biafran soldiers under the established Geneva Convention Humanitarian Rules for war.

There were a dozen Biafran POWs in the military prison, whose care she was assigned to keep tabs on. Among them was a 20-year-old prisoner of war (POW), Udochukwu Abara. Something about him stood out to her. She was so intrigued by him that she began to develop an interest in him that went beyond the scope of her official assignment as POW care observer. In a matter of weeks, she was enamored of him, and the sense of intrigue and interest would morph into a secret love relationship.

During her first weekly session with Udochukwu Abara in her office, she told him, "You remind me a lot about my late husband, both in manners and physical characteristics."

"Oh, Madam, I am sorry to hear about your loss."

"Thank you. We were young and in love. I was teaching in an elementary school in Paris. He was an accountant at a major wine distribution company in Paris. Not long after we met, we were married, and just when we were starting a new life together, tragedy struck. It was raining heavily the evening he was driving home from work. The fog in the air caused poor visibility. Unfortunately, a truck coming from the opposite direction skidded off its lane, and slammed into my husband's car in a head-on collision, killing him instantly," she said and broke down sobbing, and dabbed her eyes with a tissue.

"Madam, I am so sorry," said Udochukwu Abara, consolingly.

"That's okay. I'll be fine. Feel free to call me by my first name, Collette, okay?" she said.

She wanted him to feel comfortable and at ease with her, irrespective of her official role in the prison. Meanwhile, it was a strange new dynamic in the relationship between the two of them developing so fast, and so much so it caused the young POW to wonder what it meant in the context of his life behind the prison walls. What does this all mean? Is there something gravid with a positive outcome on the horizon for him? he thought.

During weekly sessions with each of the POW clients, Collette Durand routinely made visual inspection of their external appearance, asked them questions if anything abnormal was observed. It typically included questions about the quality of care and how prison custodial staff treated them, and if they had any concerns or worries about their incarceration and care. After Ms. Durand had signed in the Prisoner Movement Log Book maintained by the prison custodial staff at the front desk in the dormitory where Udochukwu Abara was, she took him to her office for their second weekly session. This time, she wanted to know more about the young POW. She motioned to him to sit on a two-seater couch in her office backing the wall.

"Tell me about yourself and your family. I am sure you must be missing them under the unpleasant circumstance of the war," she said.

"Indeed, I do, very much," said Udochukwu Abara, now that he was no longer feeling the kind of morbid anxiety he had in those harrowing moments after he was captured on the battle field at Abak.

When he began to narrate his story, Ms. Durand got up from her chair behind her desk, scooted over to the couch and sat next to him. As she listened, she made overtures with highly suggestive body language that unmistakably communicated her amorous feelings.

"Oh, poor baby," leaning forward, she said, and began to stroke his face with both palms of her hands and gave him a peck on the forehead. Realizing that her office door was shut but not locked, she got up and locked it to ensure full protection of their privacy.

Back on the couch, her moves were now more intense and irresistible. She slowly unbuttoned her blouse, exposing her cleavage. The young man's virility was challenged, and he just couldn't resist the force of nature in the face of incipient seduction. Testosterone kicked in and shot to its peak. She turned up the air conditioner in her office so the sound would drown out the squeaking noise of the couch as they fondled and rumbled feverishly on it. Several weeks later, Udochukwu Abara learned that he'd impregnated Collette Durand. He is overwhelmed and wondered how that could have been. Then it dawned on him that they'd had unprotected sex. The thought of what the latest development meant, in their seemingly unusual relationship, consumed his mind. What would be the back story of their meeting in the prison? Would his capture at the Abak frontline and subsequent transfer to the military prison in Calabar be seen down the line as something that serendipitously led to a positive outcome for his life? he thought, simultaneously relishing the news that he is said to be the father of the baby the French lady was carrying. He fantasized about the prospects of the new development becoming a providential ticket to his freedom. His fantasy may have seemed quixotic, but it would turn out to be, not just a wishful thinking, but something well within the realm of reality.

COLLETTE DURAND began to nurse an idea of how to get Udochukwu Abara out of prison, illegally, and take him with her to France. She told him about the idea.

"Oh, my God! Are you serious?" he asked. "How in the world would that be done?" he asked, with a stare of incredulity.

In a hushed tone, she said, "Do not worry, leave it to me. Just keep it to yourself."

Madly in love, she felt that for Udochukwu Abara, a successful escape from prison to freedom potentially would outweigh the high risk involved and would be worth it. She laid out to him her plan of action for his escape and methodically explained each step of the plot to the point of exit, including a one-way trip with her to France, where they'd start a new life, with a baby on the way. They made a covenant of secrecy, to never, under any circumstance, give off any appearance of an active love relationship between them that would raise eyebrows and trigger inquiries that could potentially uncover the plot and have very serious consequences.

Chapter 9
THE RESOURCES

THE IDEA OF A PRISON ESCAPE was a bold imagination. It would require a sophisticated plan with a fair amount of resources to effectively pull it off. Collette Durand had the right person in mind with whom she could brainstorm and explore the practicality of the idea. She contacted her best friend, Emily DuPont, back home in Paris, France. Both the same age, they go back a long way since their time together as teachers at the elementary school, where they were hired on the same day. After the tragic loss of Collette Durand's husband, and she left teaching and joined the International Green Cross, the two ladies had remained friends, and had maintained regular contact. During their long telephone chat, Collette Durand brought up Udochukwu Abara in the conversation, and shared intimate details about her relationship with him, how she met the young POW in the military prison in Calabar, Nigeria, and how her official assignment in the prison as POW care inspector went beyond the scope of her oversight responsibilities and morphed into a furtive love relationship, ultimately resulting in her pregnancy, following an affair — *one night stand* — they had in her office.

"Oh là là!" Emily bantered. "So you're pregnant

now."

"*Oui, Emily,*" said Collette.

"*Toutes nos felicitations!*"

"*Merci,*" replied Collette.

"The situation was so irresistible. Something about him that reminded me of my late husband, and before I knew it, I was falling head over heels for him."

"Totally understandable. I can appreciate that," said Emily.

"Now, here's what I want to do. I have this idea to help him get out of prison, by way of escape," said Collette Durand, as she began to narrate to her friend, an imaginary sketch of the plot she'd conceived—

"I'll have him put on the uniform of an army officer, with two stars, one on each shoulder of his uniform, depicting the rank of a 2nd Lieutenant, a belt, and a pair of officers' brown shoes. It'll include donning a soldier's hat he'll pull down to his eyebrows, also wearing very dark sunglasses to obscure his face from recognition. He'll be carrying a briefcase in his hand and walk out from the prison dormitory as if he's a real army officer leaving after a meeting with me. The prison guard at the front desk in the dormitory will stand up and give him a military salute as military protocol demands of a lower ranking personnel. Nigerians are culturally known to revere symbols of authority, and respect their superiors irrespective of age. I'll briskly follow behind him as we head toward a sidewalk that leads to the main building in the prison complex with a long hallway at the end of which there are the *'entrance and exit checkpoints'* – with long metal bars that go up — when a prison guard checks and clears a legitimate visitor coming in, and when they're leaving. He'll walk in the direction along the checkpoints to an open sideway with a posted sign that reads: **AUTHORIZED PERSONNEL ONLY.** That point will be the last obstacle to clear to get to the outside of the military prison complex."

Continuing, Collette Durand, said, "Once he's eluded the prison security guards inside and made his way to the outside, with me following behind him, we'd get into my official car waiting in front of the building. My official chauffer will take us to my apartment, less than an hour's drive away in the outskirts of Calabar town. Udochukwu Abara will remain in the back seat of the car, pretending to be reading some official document, while I walk up a flight of stairs to my apartment, grab my luggage and be back down in less than two minutes. Once my luggage is inside the car, the driver will then take us straight to Calabar airport. I know the Customs and Immigration officers at the airport. Over the course of my travels in and out of the country on assignments, I'd developed good rapport with them, always making sure I gave them gifts from my trips abroad. I believe they'll show deference to him looking like an army officer and allow him to pass through Customs and Immigration checkpoints, without asking any questions, when I tell them he's not traveling, rather only seeing me off as a friend. Once we're out of their sight, we'll walk straight to the departure hall and then head toward a small Cessna plane with the logo of International Green Cross sitting on the tarmac. The plane will be flying to Gabon, where the crew will pick up a set of International Green Cross workers going for relief assignment in another location on the Continent. I'll tell the pilot and 2 crew members of the IGC Cessna plane, both of whom already know me, that the young military officer coming on board with me, is a Nigerian army 2nd Lieutenant and military intelligence officer, who works at the military prison and is traveling with me to Gabon for a conference in connection with my oversight responsibilities on Biafran POWs in the military prison. With that introduction, they'd assume he has his traveling document with him, and in deference wouldn't bother to ask for verification. When we land in Gabon, the French speaking former colony of France on the West Coast of Africa, and one of the few African countries supporting Biafra in the Nigerian Civil War, he'll tell Gabonese Immigration officials that he's defecting from Nigeria, to voluntarily terminate his role in the military as an officer, in protest of his country's hostilities toward innocent citizens of Biafra. And that is why he wants to seek asylum in Gabon. I'll vouch for him, and claim that he and I had been close associates in the Nigerian military prison in Calabar, and that he had regularly shared with me his feelings about his country's actions toward Biafra, which he considered to be unsettling, and as a result, he decided to escape to Gabon. I believe Gabonese immigration officials will think his story is credible, empathize with him, give him the benefit of the doubt, and allow him into the country as an asylum seeker. They'll have him fill out an 'Asylum Application Form,' and provide shelter for him, probably in government housing, in Libreville, Gabon, and allow me visitation access, pending a hearing date for his Asylum Application.”

“In the interim, I’ll check into a hotel in the city and stay for a few days before flying home to Paris. When I get home, I’ll contact an immigration attorney and explore any legal means by which he can obtain a travel Visa from the French Embassy in Gabon to come to France. I suspect, a quicker and most favorable option potentially, may be for us to tie the knots in Gabon, and he can then apply for a French Visa on the basis of our marriage. In that case, I’ll fly back to Gabon and we have a courthouse marriage there. With our marriage certificate in hand, and supporting documents of sponsorship from me as his French citizen spouse, he’ll most likely get the visa. *Voila!, Ça y est!, C’est cela!, Ça suffit!, C’est tout*! In no time, we’ll be on a flight to Paris together, on Air France!”

“My goodness! What an elaborate plan, Collette. Sounds like no dry idea to me. A vivid picture of what you plan to do in precise detail.”

“The greatest challenge now, Emily, is how to get and put the different parts of the picture together to implement the plan,” said Collette.

“I hear you; I’ll talk with my husband and see what he says.”

“My husband knows someone in the African immigrant community in Paris, whom I’m sure will be up to the task. Call me, not this coming Saturday, but the next one after it, and I’ll have an answer for you, okay?”

“Oui, merci beaucoup!”

“Oh, by the way; have you told your parents or any

member of your family about this new development?"

"No, not yet. Only you, for now."

"I think it's important to let your parents know, especially the news about your pregnancy," Emily suggested.

"I agree, Emily. I plan to do so as soon as possible," said Collette, adding, "which is why I'd like to have everything about this plot put together and executed in December, around when my vacation period for the Christmas and New Year's Holidays would come up. Also, before the baby bump starts showing, and arouse the curiosity of my colleagues."

Chapter 10

EMILY'S HUSBAND, JEAN LAMBERT is a manager of a motel chain in Paris. He has a friend, who owns a fleet of French taxis operated by drivers he hires mostly from the African immigrant community. Majority of them have forged documents that look incredibly authentic. Monsieur Lambert talked to his friend, Monsieur Albert Lavage, owner of *Bonne Balade Taxi* in Paris about what Collette Durand wanted to do. Turned out Lavage had the right person for the job — a notorious kingpin of an underground enterprise involved in the production of fictitious documents, such as international passports, identification cards – and what have you. The fellow also has sewing tools and materials to produce uniforms of all kinds, sizes and shapes, including badges and insignia tailored exactly to customer's request.

When contacted and told about what Collette Durand wanted, the boss of the underworld enterprise said, "Oui, Oui, Oui…. We can do all that," and added that the prospective customer should come see him at his office to discuss in detail what they wanted. His office is located in the heart of Downtown Paris, and he goes by an alias, "Dupatta." He's said to have emigrated from Mali to France in the late 1940s as a young man in his twenties, and had worked in the fashion industry for some time, after which he opened a mini retail store selling African outfits and T-shirts with pictorial logos. The graphic impressions on the T-shirts, included images of social activists and celebrity musicians. His small business grew into an underground enterprise which produced fictitious documents for international immigrants to France, mostly from African countries, used in finding jobs, as taxi drivers and maids in motels and hotels. He's well-connected and has influential friends who are prominent public figures in the city, but goes to great lengths to keep his infamous business activities outside the eyes of the law.

Lavage gave his friend, Monsieur Lambert, the address of Dupatta's office and said he was expecting him. Lambert went with his wife, Emily to meet the notorious business tycoon. On arrival, he knocked on the front door, and within seconds, a slim, dark skinned lady, in her mid-twenties opened the door. "Hello," she said, ushering them into the building. The interior looked like a boutique shop with racks of clothing that included T-shirts, ladies' hats, bags, shoes, belts, African fashion and wigs, etc. On one corner on the floor, was her desk, a chair and a receptionist's telephone. She then led Lambert and his wife down a curved staircase to a basement floor. At the end of the stairs, they turned right and snaked through a half-lit hallway that led to Dupatta's office. She knocked on the door and announced that his visitors have arrived.

"Okay," said Dupatta.

She then turned and went back up to the main floor. Lambert and his wife stood there for almost 10 minutes without anyone coming to open the door. They were a bit flustered by the prolonged silence. Then the door was opened, and they stepped in. Standing behind a large mahogany table facing the door, was Dupatta, a short and stocky man with a rotund face and a little goatee. He had a big grin. And scooting on the far left corner behind him, was a huge, scary brown guard dog on a leash tied to a pole. The canine growled and bared its sharp, pointed vicious teeth. Dupatta raised his right hand projecting a gesture of welcome to his visitors. Just then, to the utter consternation of Lambert and his wife, two young men sprung up from behind the door, with pistols drawn standing in front of them.

"Please raise your hands," said one of the gunmen to the couple, their mouths agape, speechless and looking at Dupatta, in total shock.

"Relax, no harm intended," said Dupatta, smugly.

The couple raised their hands, and one of the gunmen did a body pat-down, one after the other to ensure they had no weapons, or any electronic recording device on them, while the other gunman had his pistol pointed at the couple. After they were patted down, and found not to have anything on them that potentially posed a threat, Dupatta motioned them to the two chairs in front of his table.

"Please sit down, don't be offended," he said. "It's a matter of security protocol," he attempted to offer an explanation.

At first, the couple's grim facial expressions showed they weren't buying Dupatta's explanation. Dupatta continued to prod them to accept the reason for the action they'd just experienced, given the nature of the business he was running. After a while, the couple came to terms with Dupatta's explanation and agreed to keep confidential, everything about their transaction with him. They told Dupatta exactly what they wanted done and the purpose, on behalf of Ms. Durand, for Udochukwu Abara, the would-be prison escapee, in the military prison in Calabar, Nigeria. Dupatta pulled out a box from the top drawer of his table containing a catalog of the jobs he'd done, and showed the couple. They were an array of international passport samples and personal identification cards – all of them forged documents — that looked every bit as authentic as the original copies juxtaposed with the fake ones. His visitors were stunned. Dupatta then listed the information he would need from them specifically with reference to the end user, the POW, Udochukwu Abara. It included—

Udochukwu Abara's passport size photo. Height. Weight. Color of eyes, hair. Size of shirt he wears (small, medium, large or extra-large; waist and length measurement of pants/trouser, including shoe size). Photo of army uniform with insignia, including belt, hat and officers' shoes, worn by army personnel in the military prison in Calabar. The list also included how much Dupatta would charge for the job.

WHEN LAMBERT AND HIS WIFE got home, they called Lavage, owner of the taxi service in Paris, who'd introduced them to Dupatta, and narrated the ordeal they went through in his office. "What a bizarre and frightening encounter it was. Why didn't you let me know we were going to experience something scary and bizarre, as part of his so called 'security protocol?" Lambert asked.

"Really? Frankly, I didn't know about that; maybe it was part of his shtick, or something, whatever that was meant to be," said Lavage.

"If not for my wife, Emily, who urged me to endure and accept the premise of what transpired, as the man himself explained to us, I was ready to end everything and never meet with him again," Lambert vented.

As promised, Emily called her friend, Collette Durand and gave her the feedback from the contact she and her husband made with the notorious business tycoon, called Dupatta, in Paris. As time was of the essence, she read to Durand over the phone, the list of items and information Dupatta said he would need, and told her the amount he'd listed as the total price for the job. Durand agreed, and said she would get to work on the list right away. Over the next couple of sessions with Udochukwu Abara, she obtained from him the relevant personal identification information as Dupatta had stipulated, and used her camera and took some photographs of him. She also approached one of the army staff she's friendly with in the military prison, and asked him to pose for photograph in his army uniform, under the pretext that she would like to have the photo for remembrance sake after leaving Nigeria. The army staff obliged and Durand took several photos of him in different poses, prominently showing the army insignia on the uniform. After she had the photo prints developed from the negatives at a local photography shop in Calabar, and made sure she got back all the originals of the negatives, she packaged the developed copies, including personal identification information of Udochukwu Abara and sent to Emily by Courier express mail. Within two days, Emily called and acknowledged receipt. The following day, she and her husband were back at Dupatta's office to deliver the package of items and information he'd asked for. They made a fifty-percent down payment towards the total price.

"Everything will be ready in one week," Dupatta told them.

Chapter 11

SURE ENOUGH IN ONE WEEK, everything was ready as Dupatta had promised. Lambert and Emily were back at Dupatta's, and inspected the items he'd produced – the green army uniform corresponding with the color of the one in the photos Durand had taken, the army hat, belt, the insignia, exactly the same, and two brown plastic stars for a 2nd Lieutenant, pair of brown shoes, dark sunglasses, and a new Nigerian Passport with Udochukwu Abara's photo under an assumed name identification listed with the rank of army 2nd Lieutenant. Everything was produced to specification as given. They paid Dupatta the balance of the price, thanked him and left.

Emily packaged the items in a box and sent to Collette Durand by courier express mail, using her office address, the *International Green Cross*, in Calabar, Nigeria. In less than 48 hours, the office mail clerk delivered the box to Durand. She opened the box, and was so riveted by the things she saw. Breathing a sigh of relief, she emoted: "One major step down, a few more to go!"

COLLETTE DURAND'S PREGNANCY was in the early stages of development. She was hoping to put off prenatal care until she was back home in France. So her pregnancy situation now created a sense of urgency around the need to execute the plot that would enable Udochukwu Abara to escape from the military prison in Calabar, and ultimately travel with her to France. Their love relationship was still strictly under the radar. In her job she regularly met with the other Biafran POWs separated from each other in different units of the prison dormitories. But relative to the others, Durand's affection for Udochukwu Abara influenced her pattern of work behavior, which was ostensibly favorable toward him than the rest of his fellow POW inmates. She spent more time meeting with Udochukwu during their weekly sessions than she did with the others. Shortly after she'd received the items from her friend Emily in France, she met with Abara and told him about the good news.

"One major step down, a few more to go," she elatedly whispered in his ears during her weekly session with him. "With everything working out as planned hopefully, we'd spend Christmas and New Year's together in France and thereafter," she said. "I'll layout the plan, and we'll go through each step carefully, so you know exactly what to do, and how to act each step of the way," she reiterated, adding, "I know it's a major undertaking, inherently scary and will make you feel perhaps more nervous than ever. But, you'd been a soldier under much stressful situations. We can't afford to let your anxiety show and potentially cause any suspicion or apprehension. This is your one and only best chance to begin the journey to your freedom, and we must make it through to the finish line, without a hitch!"

Udochukwu Abara felt the weight of mixed

emotions on his mind. As tears slowly filled his eyes, Collette Durand stood up and asked him to stand and come closer to her. She took his right hand and placed his palm on her belly, and tenderly rubbed it in a circular motion for a few seconds.

"The step we are about to take for your freedom, in a significant way, is for your baby inside of me, our baby, I should say," she said softly, and gave him a peck on the forehead.

After a couple of meetings they had in her office behind closed doors, and furtively rehearsed what was going to be done, they were ready to put the plan into action.

Chapter 12
ACTION DAY

LUCKILY, COLLETTE DURAND'S OFFICE is located in a wing of office units adjacent to the building housing the dormitory where Udochukwu Abara is kept. The proximity worked to their advantage. At eight in the morning on a Friday, she arrived for work, carrying with her a briefcase and a medium size suitcase. The suitcase contained everything about the outfit of a military officer Udochukwu Abara was going to wear. She stopped at the front desk in the dormitory section of the building that is structurally connected to her office through a hallway door.

"Good morning, John," she greeted the guard on duty.

"Good Morning, Madam," replied the guard. "I want to let you know that I'll be going on vacation for the upcoming Christmas and New Year's holidays and probably won't see you again for the rest of the week before I leave."

"Oh, Madam. We will miss you. Merry Christmas and Happy New Year to you in advance."

"Merci beaucoup, John. I wish you and your family the same in advance," said Ms. Durand. "Oh, I like to have a session with Udochukwu Abara after their lunch around 2:00 p.m., since I'll be on vacation for a while. So please tell him to come to my office at two."

"Okay, Madam. I will tell him," said the guard.

"Also, I'll be meeting this afternoon with an army officer, a 2nd Lieutenant from the office of military intelligence in my office. He may come when you're in the dining hall with the inmates, and probably have the key to get into the dormitory. Just so you are aware, in case you see him leaving with me after our meeting," said Durand.

"Okay, Madam. No problem."

At 2:00 p.m., Udochukwu Abara came to Durand's office. After about forty minutes, she locked the door, and had him take off the white and black stripes POW uniform he was wearing, and put on the army uniform she'd brought. From head to toe, Udochukwu Abara looked every bit a military officer, dressed like a real army 2nd Lieutenant. He had the hat pulled down to his eyebrows and donned the dark sunglasses. He put the POW uniform inside the suitcase, but didn't zip up the suitcase properly. Collette, for the first time, donned a white beret with the embroidered insignia of International Green Cross. At 3:00 p.m., after pausing for a moment of silence in prayer, they stepped out of Durand's office, and she locked the door. Udochukwu Abara was carrying the suitcase by the handle, and Collette Durand was carrying the briefcase. They walked down the hallway through the door into the dormitory wing of the building and turned left toward the front desk. Abara is completely disguised in the army uniform he was wearing. The hat, pulled down to his eyebrows, and the dark sunglasses covering his eyes, obscured his face from recognition.

"Oh, Madam, you're leaving now?" said the dormitory guard, getting up from his chair at the front desk to go unlock the exit door for Durand and Abara, disguised as an army officer.

The prison guard thought that Udochukwu Abara had gone back to his corner in the dormitory after meeting with Ms. Durand. He was wrong. Unknown to him, the person he thought was a 2nd Lieutenant, was POW Udochukwu Abara.

"Yes, John," replied Durand. While John, the prison guard headed to unlock the exit door, Durand set down her briefcase on the floor by the front desk, and said to Abara, "Go ahead, Officer, let me take a moment and sign the IN & OUT *Inmates Movement Log Book* that I forgot to sign before and after my meeting with POW Udochukwu Abara this afternoon."

As Abara walked toward the exit door, the prison guard stepped aside and gave Udochukwu Abara a military salute deserving of a superior officer. Abara simply nodded. The nonverbal gesture with only a nod of the head didn't seem to register well with the guard, sneering inaudibly as he walked back to the front desk, "What arrogance! He didn't even bother to reciprocate my salute the military way; what kind of training did he receive at the Nigerian Defense Academy?"

Nigerian Defense Academy, generally referred to as NDA, the country's top officer cadet training institution in Kaduna.

Durand gave the guard a hug and exchanged parting pleasantries, while Udochukwu Abara, his heart pounding, was already standing outside the dormitory door. Once Durand came out, they used the sidewalk that looped around the sprawling landscape of the facility to get to the big building, where the main entrance and exit checkpoints are located. Durand occasionally glanced behind her shoulders to see if anyone was hastily coming after them. It'd be a few more hours before the inmates go to the dining hall for their supper. Along the way on the sidewalk, Abara accidentally had a misstep and fell, tripping over the suitcase he was carrying that was not properly zipped up. It was a hair-raising moment, when his POW uniform inside the suitcase spilled onto the sidewalk. Collette Durand instantly lurched forward and grabbed the suitcase. She stuffed the POW uniform back into the suitcase and zipped it up properly. Luckily no one else was around to notice the tension driven sidewalk mishap.

"Are you okay, Officer?" said Durand, pretending to sound sympathetic. "Be careful, Officer," she said, when Abara got up and they continued toward the main building, where the final exit point was.

FROM THE SIDEWALK, they veered left to another pathway that took them into the main building. "Slow down," said Durand, once they were inside the main building.

Walking side by side and pretending to be chatting, but Durand, the one only doing the talking, she reminded Abara to stay to the right and go through the open side at the last checkpoint toward the main exit, with a sign that reads: *AUTHORIZED PERSONNEL ONLY.*

It was now almost twenty minutes past three in the afternoon since they left the dormitory block, where

Udochukwu Abara had stayed as a POW for the last four months. Getting through the last exit checkpoint was going to be consequential. The prison guard supervisor at the counter overseeing the entry and exit checkpoints noticed Collette Durand and said, "Oh, Madam, so you're leaving now, I suppose. We will surely miss you."

Durand waved at Abara and said, "Officer, you go ahead, I'll be with you in a minute. Let me say goodbye to my friends over here."

She leaned over to hug the head prison guard and exchange parting pleasantries with him and the other guards, so that their inattention at that moment would make it easier for Abara to walk through without being noticed. But Udochukwu Abara fumbled. Instead of going through the open side lane designated for AUTHORIZED PERSONNEL ONLY as Collette Duran had reminded him to do just moments earlier, he proceeded to go through the lane of the exit checkpoint for visitors with the metal barrier across. Luckily, the guard at the checkpoint, in deference to him thinking he's a real army officer, stood at attention, gave him a military salute, and lifted the metal barrier for him to pass through. Udochukwu Abara remained mute as he walked through and never saluted back, in a military fashion.

"He didn't have to come through this lane, he should've used the open lane for authorized personnel only," said the guard, chuckling, looking at his fellow guards.

Abara had raised eyebrows among the prison guards, who were ostensibly wondering if he was a legitimate army officer working at the facility, and ought to know better. Collette Duran had caught the snafu, too and cringed, as Abara made the unforced error that could have bollixed-up the entire plot, potentially with grave consequences. She waved goodbye to the prison guards and quickly moved on to exit the building.

Chapter 13

"THANK GOD!" said Durand when she got outside and saw Udochukwu Abara standing on the curb in front of the building.

Durand's assigned chauffer was sitting in the white Peugeot 404 official car she uses, waiting for her. She looked up and waved at him. He pulled up by the curb where Durand and Abara were standing. Durand opened the rear door and got in with Abara. The driver took off and turned right at the main gate of the military prison onto Hope Waddell Road. Shortly afterwards, the two-way traffic road merged into a single lane traffic due to construction work. Traffic was crawling. Durand glanced at her wrist watch and rolled her eyes.

"Oh, Lord," she murmured, knitting her brows.

"Why didn't you go the opposite direction? You should've turned left at the gate and taken the other route to my place to avoid this traffic jam," she said.

To absolve himself from blame, the driver politely responded, "Madam, we didn't know about this construction. It wasn't like this in the morning when we came. They must have started the construction this afternoon."

Luckily, the traffic slow down didn't last long. By about 4:30 p.m., they got to Durand's flat (apartment building). She got out and ran up a flight of stairs to her unit. Within minutes, she was back down carrying another suitcase and a backpack. As soon as the luggage was loaded in the truck, the driver took off and they were on their way to Calabar airport. They arrived the airport around 5:15 p.m. Durand tipped the driver with *10 Pounds, Nigerian currency,* and they bade goodbye. She had her International Green Cross band visibly worn around her arm and donning the white beret as she and Udochukwu Abara, still in the army uniform with the rank of 2nd Lieutenant, walked into the airport and proceeded towards Customs and Immigration checkpoints. She was carrying one suitcase and her backpack slung over her left shoulder. Udochukwu Abara was carrying a brief case and the other suitcase, inside of which was his POW uniform.

As planned, with an air of cheerfulness, Collette Duran struck up a conversation with the Customs and Immigration officers, who already know her, telling them she was traveling home to France on vacation for the upcoming Christmas and New Year's holidays, and added: "Oh, this is 2nd Lieutenant John Bode, a friend who works at the military prison with me. He's not traveling he's just seeing me off."

They naively believed her and obliged without checking the luggage Abara was carrying, including hers, and only stamped "Departure" on her passport and waved both of them on. 5:40 p.m., they rustled to the departure hall, which had not a whole lot of travelers, most of them expatriates. Durand and Abara proceeded cautiously through a narrow gate, trying not to invite any attention by avoiding eye contacts with other passengers. Anyone among the waiting passengers in the departure hall, who knew Collette Durand, could come up to her to say hello and strike up a chat, she thought, and wanted to evade that chance as much as possible. Soon they were on the tarmac. The International Green Cross small 8-seater Cessna plane, scheduled to fly to Gabon, was sitting on the tarmac, a short distance away. They briskly walked to the plane. The pilot and two crew members knew Collette Durand and were expecting her. But not the man dressed in army uniform with the rank of 2nd Lieutenant.

"This is Officer John Bode," said Collette Durand to the flight crew, introducing Udochukwu Abara, with an alias. "2nd Lieutenant Bode is traveling with me to Gabon. We work together at the military prison in Calabar. He is a military intelligence officer overseeing our work with the POWs, and he was asked by the director of the military prison at the last minute to travel to Gabon for a related conference. So by happenstance, he's catching the flight with me to Gabon."

Given how close and friendly Durand was with the pilot and the two crew members; with no questions asked, they obliged and welcomed Udochukwu Abara, *"aka army 2nd Lieutenant John Bode"* aboard with open arms. At 6:00 p.m., the pilot started the engine. Everyone's seatbelt was fastened. Soon the International Green Cross Cessna plane rumbled along the tarmac for takeoff. At 6:05 p.m., it was airborne, and Udochukwu Abara had made a daring escape from the dungeon of captivity to the blue skies of freedom.

Chapter 14

THE PLANE WAS HALF-FILLED. Collette Durand and Udochukwu Abara sat in the back so they could relax and chat without being heard by the flight crew sitting in the front end closer to the cockpit.

"Here, look…look… the military prison below," Durand said to Abara.

He got up slightly from his aisle seat, took off the dark sunglasses, and leaning over Durand's shoulder, he peered down the right hand side of the plane and took a bird's eye view of the prison below, as they flew over the place he'd been held in captivity as a prisoner of war for the last four months. It was an incredible view. It felt surreal. He couldn't believe he was out of the four walls of the military prison and on to freedom. It was just about dinner time, when the inmates would be gathering in the dining hall. They both wondered at that moment; what would be the reaction of John, the prison guard in the dormitory, when Udochukwu Abara was not seen in the dining hall with the rest of the inmates? His absence would trigger a lockdown of the facility and a manhunt would ensue, they speculated. It would become a major news story in the media, and the impact of the resulting embarrassment would be felt across military establishments in Calabar and in Lagos.

After having anxiety suppressing food appetite during those tense moments of maneuvering the escape from the military prison, Collette Durand and Udochukwu Abara were naturally hungry and ready to eat again, albeit on freedom's flight at 20,000 feet in the air. The crew had offered them a light meal that included ham and chicken sandwich, with potato chips and some cans of Coca Cola and Fanta soft drinks. Feeling relaxed and comfortable, they ate with a healthy appetite. The flight to Gabon took less than two hours. Upon landing at Gabon International Airport, Durand and Abara disembarked and quickly headed to the arrival hall to go through arrival formalities at Gabon Immigration post before the Cessna flight crew would come along. Durand didn't want them to see her and Abara being questioned by Immigration officials, as that might tip off the real circumstance surrounding Abara's flight to Gabon. So, luckily they didn't stand on the line for arriving passengers going through immigration formalities for too long. Durand was first to be seen with her passport duly stamped, for arrival into the country with no questions asked. Right before it got to Abara's turn, she pulled the attending immigration officer aside, and said that there was a unique situation with the passenger in a military officer's uniform behind her. She said, he came on the same flight with her from Nigeria, and essentially to seek asylum in Gabon. The attending immigration officer asked her who she was. She introduced herself. Then the immigration officer picked up the phone on the counter in front of him and called his boss and told him about Abara's situation. He hung up the phone, and asked another officer to take Durand and Abara to the office of the assistant director of Immigration Service, on the 6th floor of the airport's Administration Building. They got into an elevator, and as it went up, Collette Durand trained her eyes on the blinking light buttons inching nearer to floor number 6.

"Madam, I learn that the young military officer you arrived with from Nigeria wants to seek asylum in Gabon," said the assistant director of Gabon Immigration Service at the airport, after a brief introduction.

"That's correct, Sir," said Durand.

She proceeded to narrate to the assistant director, the circumstances that led them to Gabon, and essentially made the point that Udochukwu Abara, referred to as 2nd Lieutenant John Bode, had defected from the Nigeria Army as a conscientious objector to the ongoing Nigeria Biafra Civil War, in protest of what he believed the Nigerian side was doing against Biafra that was inhumane. She added that her involvement in Abara's situation was solely on humanitarian grounds. Being that Gabon was one of a handful of African countries that had taken a foreign policy stance in recognition and support of Biafra, the assistant director of immigration was receptive and commended Abara, noting that he was ballsy in doing what he did, which was admirable. He assured that they would grant him asylum. Durand blinked her eyes and winked at Udochukwu Abara with a smile.

"We will have him fill out the Application for Asylum Form, process it and give him a hearing date to see an immigration judge," said the immigration boss.

"Just for formality as official protocol requires. I know he'll get the asylum status, and with that he'll be eligible for a work permit, so he can get employment in the country and support himself," he added.

As if on cue, Collette and Durand both said at the same time, "Thank you, Sir!"

That was the first time Abara said something, in many hours since they left Durand's office in the military prison in Calabar. "We can't thank you enough! Merci Beaucoup," added Durand.

Just as they were about to leave the immigration boss's office, he said, "Oh, by the way… I forgot to tell you that in the meantime, after his application for asylum has been processed and a hearing date given, he'd be taken to a government housing accommodation here in Libreville, where he'd stay until the day he'd see the immigration judge. I don't know what your travel itinerary is, but I am told that your passport shows you're a French citizen. I am assuming you may be traveling on to France. Nonetheless, if you do decide to stay a few more days in Gabon, you are welcome to do so and will have access to the place the young military officer cum asylum seeker will be staying."

"Okay, Madam, nice meeting you. My officer here who brought you up to see me, will take you two to the office where *2nd Lieutenant John Bode* will fill out the application form for asylum and submit for processing," said the immigration assistant director with a grin.

As Durand and Abara were being led to the office

where Abara would fill out the application for asylum form, Durand pondered whether or not to divulge to Gabon immigration authorities, Udochukwu Abara's real identity, as a native of Biafra, who was captured on the battle field and sent to a military prison in Calabar, Nigeria, where they met in the course of her job with the International Green Cross. She decided to hold off yet. It was well late into the night by the time the application process for asylum was completed and a hearing date – in 2 months' time – was given.

The immigration officers assisted Durand with finding a hotel. Two officers drove Durand and Abara in an official Gabon Immigration Service van, first to the government funded housing location in the city, where Abara was given temporary accommodation. Then they drove Durand to the hotel, where she checked in, and would stay for the next few days. She was elated, couldn't believe how well the plan had worked out so far. She couldn't wait to tell her best friend Emily. It was around midnight in Gabon, when Emily would be waking up in France. She allowed a couple of hours to elapse, then called Emily.

"Hello, Emily dear. Bonjour. Guess what!" she said boisterously. "We made it! He is out, and we're in Libreville, Gabon now!"

"Bonjour, Collette. Congratulations!" said Emily.

"I know you're just getting up, it's been a long, harrowing day. I just checked into a hotel. Midnight now. A lot to unpack and tell you about when we speak. Let me try and get some sleep. We shall talk, my friend," said Collette.

Chapter 15

THE PHONE IN COLLETTE DURAND'S HOTEL ROOM rang. It was Saturday, around 10 o'clock in the morning. Still in bed and worn-out from the day before, coupled with insufficient sleep, she rolled over, stretched out an arm and picked up the phone. "Hello," she drawled, half asleep.

"Hello, good morning Madam. It's me, the assistant director of immigration. How are you doing, everything okay?"

"Oh, yes, yes, yes. I remember you. I'm fine, just that I'm still asleep after the exhaustion from yesterday," said Durand, wondering how the immigration boss knew where she was and called her. "Must have been his junior officers, who dropped her off at the hotel last night," she thought.

"Oh, I'm sorry. I can understand. It was pretty late last night when my officers drove you and the asylum seeker to where he's being accommodated, and dropped you off at your hotel."

"Yes, indeed. It was pretty late last night when we left."

"I was wondering, if you might be interested in meeting later today, say in the evening, for dinner at one of the finest restaurants here in Libreville. We can chat over the asylum matter for the young

69

military officer. His hearing date is coming up in two months' time, but I can leverage my position to have him seen by the immigration judge a lot sooner, and facilitate the process of granting him the asylum."

"Oh, that is so kind of you, Sir. I don't know, I'm still sleepy right now. Maybe I can get back to you in an hour?" said Durand.

"Okay, no problem. That'll be fine," said the immigration boss. "Oh, no!" he groaned, after he'd hung up and realized he did not leave Durand with his telephone number where he could be reached. He quickly called back the hotel, and asked the receptionist to give his phone number to Ms. Durand. The hotel receptionist called Durand and gave her the phone number as instructed.

Collette Durand suddenly became fully awake. She started brooding over the call from the immigration boss. What must have caused him to call? He sounded like there was something else that motivated him to call her, as the sultry tone of his voice ostensibly suggested, she thought. Since she had the sneaky suspicion that he might be on to something couched in an evening social get-together he'd proposed, she wondered if she should thank him for his invitation, but decline the offer. Or, if she should call him back and accept to meet with him for the evening social get-together, but muster the courage to tell him that she was in a serious relationship at the moment, and pregnant, once he started to drift in an unbecoming direction. She weighed the latter option against the risk of potentially making the immigration boss feel disappointed and potentially jeopardize the prospects of a favorable outcome in Udochukwu Abara's application for asylum. She struggled with what all that could possibly mean. The conundrum likely to result from the situation necessitated a call to her best friend, Emily in Paris.

When Collette Durand called Emily shortly after the brief phone conversation she had with the immigration boss, she gave Emily a complete rundown of how everything went with Udochukwu Abara, regarding how they maneuvered the escape – from the military prison in Calabar, Nigeria — to Gabon International Airport. She told her about the latest knotty issue she perceived from her phone conversation a short while ago, with the immigration boss, inviting her out to dinner. She mentioned that it felt like the invitation may have some underlying motive with strings attached, and she needed her wise counsel.

"Okay, here's what I'll suggest you do," Emily began. "When you call him back, tell him you appreciate his thoughtfulness and that you accept his kind invitation. While you two are chatting over the course of the dinner, be diplomatic and play it nice with him. Pay attention to his words, and particularly to his nonverbal behavior. Let the visual cues you pick up guide your conversation. Be nuanced with your choice of words when responding to his questions, and at the same time, be coy in responding to questions you deem too personal. Shower him with plaudits for his help so far, and particularly for the offer he'd purportedly made to move up the hearing date for the asylum application. Do not give him any impression that might lead him to think that what brought you to him was anything but a chance meeting, predicated upon the circumstance of Udochukwu Abara's flight to Gabon, and legitimate need for asylum. In fact, do not hesitate to let him know, albeit in a tactful way, about your professional status as a member of a globally recognized international humanitarian organization that deals with world leaders. In doing so, he'd know that you were no ordinary traveler on a flight to Gabon the day you arrived, and that you do hold some sway, too as a public figure in that respect. He'd be cautious, knowing that any wrong move on his part with inappropriately conceived social intent, could backfire on him and have grave implications for his career and the image of his office. Ask if he could take you to go see Udochukwu Abara. In the meantime, I think you should plan on leaving Gabon soon, say by Monday or Tuesday to come home to Paris, and then see an immigration attorney, to find out how you can legally bring Abara to France, since that's your ultimate goal."

"Isn't this amazing? You always seem to have the right answer for me. This is what best friends are for, Emily. Your insights make a whole lot of sense. Merci beaucoup," said Collette Durand.

Around 11:30 a.m., Durand called the immigration boss as promised. He was delighted Duran called back. They agreed to meet at 4:30 p.m. The immigration boss would send his driver to pick her up. At 3:45 p.m., the driver arrived at the hotel in a brown French luxury automobile, *Citröen*. Dressed in a nice outfit appropriate to go out for dinner, Collette Duran was waiting in the lobby of the hotel. The driver came into the lobby, and instinctively recognized Duran as the lady he'd come to pick up.

"You're the driver sent by the immigration boss?" asked Durand.

"Yes, Madam."

"Okay, nice to meet you," said Durand politely, as she got into the back seat of the car.

4:00 p.m. at the dot, they were at a 5-star luxury hotel in Libreville with scenic views on the coast of the city. The driver pulled up in front of the hotel. Durand got out and walked through the sliding glass entry doors into the hotel lobby. The immigration boss, already in the lobby, noticed Duran, walked up and greeted her with a handshake.

"Nice to see you again, Madam," he said. "Likewise," said Duran.

Walking side by side, a hotel staff led them to the restaurant on the ground floor with an elegant interior. They were quickly seated by a waitress who presented them with copies of the food menu, and asked what kind of drinks they'd like to have. After a brief look, they made their choices, and shortly thereafter, the waitress came back with a tray containing the meals they'd ordered, including the wines, Chardonnay and Sauvignon. Over the course of the rich and delicious meals they had, including carrot cake and chocolate ice cream, for dessert; the immigration boss, in Durand's assessment, was a perfect gentleman. The conversation they had was decent and normal, focusing mainly on the story that led Udochukwu Abara, whom the immigration boss consistently referred to as *2nd Lieutenant John Bode,* to Gabon seeking asylum. "We really admire and applaud him for his courage, in defecting," said the immigration boss. "I wish there were many like him in the military who'd be as ballsy and do what he did," he added, and noted, "that kind of action undertaken as a conscientious objector, would put tremendous pressure on the government to stop the war."

"Hahahaha… Don't you think that such an act replicated by a large swath of soldiers, if caught, would lead to court-martial for treason?" Durand quipped.

"Well, it takes self-conviction, faith and courage to initiate change for moral rectitude in society, especially if you look at what's happening in Africa and looming on the horizon," said the top immigration officer.

"I agree," said Durand.

Several times during their conversation, she was tempted to blow the cover of Abara's fake identity, but didn't. Not time yet to reveal his true identity as a Biafran soldier captured and jailed as a prisoner of war in a military prison in Calabar, Nigeria.

"I'll have my driver take you to where the Nigerian young military officer is staying, before he drops you off at your hotel," offered the immigration boss.

"Oh, that is so kind of you, thank you very much. You are such a perfect gentleman and a wonderful public figure serving the government of Gabon with honor and integrity," Durand expressed her gratitude and gave him accolades.

It was almost 6:00 p.m. by the time they left the restaurant and walked to the lobby, where the driver was waiting. The driver then left, and got the car from the parking lot and pulled up in front of the hotel. Duran shook hands with the immigration boss, thanked him and stepped down the stairs to the waiting car. She got into the back seat, and the driver took off, first to the temporary public housing accommodation where Udochukwu Abara was staying. They were so delighted to see each other. Abara seemed relieved and doing okay, Durand observed. He was staying in a small single room, furnished with a bed, desk and chair, as the only occupant. By far, the military prison dormitory, where he'd stayed as a prisoner of war in Calabar, Nigeria in the last four months, paled in comparison. He was wearing a blue cotton men's short sleeve shirt on a khaki trouser, and leather sandals, as part of a couple of civilian outfits the staff at the temporary housing facility gave him, the morning after his arrival, courtesy of Gabon's Office of Public Assistance. The army uniform he wore from the time they left the military prison in Calabar, Nigeria, was hanging in the small open closet. It was remarkable that at critical junctures of their journey from Nigeria, their suitcases were never opened for Custom's inspection, at the Calabar Airport and at Gabon International Airport. From the time they arrived and Durand notified the attending Gabon Immigration Officer processing arriving passengers, of Abara's unique arrival circumstance and request for asylum, they were both taken to the immigration boss's office, a move that resulted in bypassing Custom's inspection of their luggage. So the suitcase Udochukwu Abara was carrying, which had his assigned POW outfit in it all along, remained unopened until he was situated in the temporary housing accommodation.

Durand chuckled, when she saw the fake army uniform hanging in the closet, and wondered what they were going to do with it and the POW uniform. Perhaps the immigration boss would have an idea on how to dispose of the outfits, after she might have eventually revealed the real identity of Udochukwu Abara and the true story of how they got to Gabon, Duran thought. Meanwhile, since the driver was outside waiting, there was no time to have a prolonged chitchat, Durand said, letting Abara know that the immigration boss had been kind enough to ask his driver to bring her over to see him. She told him she'd make a reservation on Air France to fly home on Monday or Tuesday. And she'd arranged to come back probably before the hearing date for his application for asylum. She got up from the chair. Abara did, too from the edge of the single iron spring bed he was sitting on. Durand took his right hand and rubbed her tummy in a circular motion. They hugged and kissed, and before she left, she reached into her wallet and brought out some cash, in the local currency, and gave to Abara.

"Pocket money for you, till I see you again. *Être un bon garçon* (Be a good boy)," she said with a smile, and they bade goodbye.

Collette Durand got back to her hotel around 7:30 p.m. It was an evening she felt was well spent with the immigration boss, who turned out to be a perfect gentleman, contrary to what she'd initially thought of him. She'd misjudged the cadence of his voice in the way he spoke on telephone. In the hotel lobby, Durand scoured the newsstands for local and foreign newspapers that might have news about Udochukwu Abara's escape from the Calabar military prison in Nigeria. She found one in the foreign news section of a British newspaper, *London Evening Post:* *"BIAFRAN PRISONER OF WAR UNACCOUNTED FOR IN NIGERIAN MILITARY PRISON; JAILBREAK SUSPECTED!"* She picked up the paper, paid for it at the reception desk, and held her breath as she read the story riding the elevator to her hotel room on the 6th floor. *"The absence of the POW in the dining hall and dormitory for several hours, created a pandemonium, prompting a massive manhunt, both inside and outside the surrounding areas of the military prison, in Calabar, Nigeria,"* the newspaper story said. It added that, *"Extensive interviews of inmates and prison guards by authorities yielded no clues, and the whereabouts of the missing POW remained elusive. So far, no evidence found to suggest that suicide or homicide may have occurred. In the wake of the security breach and the resulting huge embarrassment for the army, Col. Haruna Abubakar, the director of the military prison and his deputy, Lt. Col. Roland Ohiro, were both demoted and relieved of their positions. They were replaced by Col. Joe Idiong, appointed as the new director, and Lt. Col. Timothy Abiodun as deputy director."*

Collette Durand was at least relieved to see that there was no mention or any speculations in the story linking her name to the presumed POW escapee, since she was technically, the last person with whom he had met for her weekly sessions with POW inmates on Friday. She folded the newspaper and tucked it away in her suitcase. It'd be a souvenir of sort she'd take home to Paris.

Chapter 16

SUNDAY MORNING AFTER BREAKFAST, Collette Duran had the staff on duty at the reception desk connect her to Air France office in the city to make a flight reservation. She booked her flight to Paris Nord International Airport for Monday, the next day departing Libreville, Gabon at 10:45 p.m. With not much left to do before her flight to Paris Monday night, she had quite a bit of time left to kill. So she called her best friend, Emily. They had a long conversation during which she told Emily all about her dinner outing the day before with the Gabon Immigration boss. And how he turned out to be a perfect gentleman, who genuinely cared about Udochukwu Abara, and was interested in his asylum case with no strings attached, with reference to his social get-together for dinner.

"That was nice of him," said Emily.

"Then, would you know it?" interjected Durand, excitedly. "I picked up a British newspaper yesterday from the newsstands here in the hotel, and read a news story about the escape of Udochukwu Abara from the military prison. The story said, after he was not seen in the dining hall and dormitory for several hours, prison officials suspected jailbreak, and began a massive manhunt in and outside the prison. I was relieved to note that nowhere in the story was my name or any speculation raised about my last official contact with him on Friday."

"Quite interesting," said Emily. "And by the way, my husband was so delighted when I told him that you two made it out precisely as planned."

"We owe your husband a huge debt of gratitude for his connections that materially aided the success of the plan," said Durand, and added, "but please tell him to keep it confidential just yet, in case he feels the urge to let his friend, Monsieur Lavage know. I wouldn't want word to get back to the notorious kingpin, Dupatta about the success of the escape, for fear he might use it as a storyline to brag to unsuspecting customers, about the collection of works he'd done, as he did indiscreetly, when you and your husband met with him in his office."

"You're right about that. I'll let him know," assured Emily.

"I have booked my flight to Paris on Air France for tomorrow, Monday. It leaves at 10:45 p.m. Gabon time," said Durand.

"Excellent!" said Emily. "I can't believe how everything seems to be working out flawlessly. It feels like the plot of a movie being played out in real time. I can't wait to see you, Collette. Bon Voyage!"

After they hung up, Collette Durand called the immigration boss and told him she'd be leaving for France the next day. "I booked a flight on Air France. It leaves tomorrow night at 10:45."

"Oh, really? My assumption was you'd stay for a few more days."

"No, I wish I could; some important things at home I have to take care of."

"We'll miss you. You know the hearing date for the young army officer's asylum case comes up in a month. But I'll try and have a new date fixed that would be a lot sooner, say in two weeks," said the immigration boss.

"Oh, my goodness! That would be great, if you could do that," Durand, excitedly blared.

"And, I can have my driver take you to the airport when you're leaving," offered the immigration boss.

"What can I say? It's so wonderful of you."

"Call me in a week, and I'll let you know a new hearing date for the asylum case, okay?"

"I'll definitely call you. Again, Merci beaucoup!" said Durand, warmly expressing her appreciation.

"Pas du tout," (not at all), said the immigration boss.

COLLETTE DURAND HAD HER LUGGAGE PACKED and ready to go. At 10:00 p.m., the driver, courtesy of the immigration boss was at the hotel. Durand came down to the reception desk and checked out. The driver put her luggage into the back of a white Peugeot 404 Station Wagon with Government vehicle plate number. Durand got in, and the driver took off to the airport. When they got to the airport, it was *VIP* treatment for Durand, who at the direction of the immigration boss, by-passed the normal baggage checking formalities with Immigration and Customs. She didn't stay in the departure lounge for too long before boarding time was announced. After boarding, the Air France commercial jetliner pulled out of its gate exactly as scheduled and taxied down the runway ready for Control Tower's clearance for takeoff. Within minutes, it roared off into the night sky glistening with stars, en route to Paris Nord International Airport.

After the dinner outing with the immigration boss Saturday evening, Collette had called her parents and told them she was coming home on leave, but had to stop over in Gabon on a work related business for a few days. Shortly before boarding the airplane, she'd called again to let them know they'd be departing soon, and the expected arrival time in Paris. Her elder sister, Marie, 35, a nurse, also aware of her trip, would be coming to pick her up from the airport. The flight arrived on schedule. Marie was already in the arrival hall, and spotted Collette. The two sisters hugged and made their way to the airport parking lot, where Marie's car was parked. Within an hour, they arrived at their parent's home in the outskirts of Paris. Marie hung out for a little while before she left and drove back home to her husband and two young children, a boy and a girl. Collette Durand chatted with her parents and got herself reacclimatized to the home she lived in growing up, and would be staying for the next few weeks. Her mom had hastily arranged a family dinner to include Collette Durand's elder sister, the nurse and her husband with their two children; her eldest sibling and only brother, Pierre, 40, single and a professor of economics at a city university in Paris. All family members had arrived in the evening for the dinner, in honor of Collette Durand back home to Paris. While Collette was in the kitchen assisting her mom put finishing touches to the delicious foods soon to be served, her dad sat in the living room with her economics professor brother, and her sister and her husband, eating mixed nuts and chips, as they watched the evening news on television, and chatted over local and international issues of the day. Then came the topic of a news story about Nigeria, Collette overheard her brother Pierre mention, which caught her attention—

"A British newspaper, this past weekend reported that a Biafran prisoner of war, was declared missing from the military prison, where he was being held, in a city called Calabar, Southeast of Nigeria," said Pierre, adding, "the news story stated that a massive manhunt that was launched in the wake of the missing POW, had not been fruitful. So far, no trace of his whereabouts."

Collette Durand's face fell, with an unmistakable sudden change in her facial expression.

"What's the matter?" asked her mom, standing next to her.

She quickly excused herself and went to the bathroom. She looked in the mirror as tears welled up in her eyes. She turned on the faucet and washed her face with cold water. When she heard her mom announce that dinner was ready, she came out of the bathroom and assisted her mom to get the foods to the table.

"Are you okay? You looked worried a moment ago," said her mom.

"I'm fine."

The delicious foods consisted of some traditional French dishes— "Salmon En Papillote. Boeuf Bourguignon. Quiche Lorraine. Potatoes Dauphinoise," and salads.

Once the dishes were out on the table, and

everyone was seated, Collette's dad, sitting at the head of the table, said a prayer before they started serving themselves, one after the other. Her brother Pierre, the economics professor, just couldn't resist the urge to bring up the news about the missing Biafran POW he read about in a British newspaper. No sooner had they started eating, than he injected the topic into a dinner conversation others at the table were having about the upcoming French presidential election. He seemed deliberately intent on eliciting Collette's take on the Nigerian story. But Collette was evasive and tried to change the subject by asking her sister Marie, something about the candidates running for the presidential election. Collette knew she was personally connected to the Nigerian news story. At that moment, she wasn't yet prepared to introduce the subject of what she had in mind to share with the family, which in many respects, was central to the Nigerian news story Pierre had alluded to. She held off until after dinner.

Chapter 17

THEY WERE DRINKING COFFEE AND TEA after having dessert, when Collette said to her mom that she had something to tell them about her trip to Nigeria, and the mission she was involved in as a member of the International Green Cross. She narrated how she'd come in contact with a young Biafran soldier named Udochukwu Abara, who was captured at the Ikot Ekpene sector of the war, South East of Nigeria, and was transferred to a military prison in Calabar, where he was being held as a prisoner of war. It was in the course of her work at the military prison, as an international observer monitoring how captured Biafran POWs were being treated, under the Geneva Convention of the rules of war that she met Udochukwu Abara. She routinely conducted weekly sessions with Abara and a few other Biafran POWs. Something about Udochukwu Abara stood out to her during the first session she had with him.

"Something so captivating and overpowering," she said, using hand gesture for dramatic effect as she passionately told her story. "He exhibited features in physical appearance and mannerism that made him look like a carbon copy of my late husband," she said. "Attributes that strangely reminded me of my husband, so much so that before I knew it, I was falling in love with him. It was so intense that before long, we had an affair and I became pregnant."

Every other member of the family at the table listened with rapt attention, showed respect for her feelings, and sympathized with her. But not her brother, Pierre, the economics professor—

"What?" said Pierre, pounding his hands on the table. "You had an affair with a young black man in Nigeria? What in the world were you thinking? I can't believe I heard you say, in essence that based on personal feelings of *love in the heat of war,* you decided on a whim to subvert the integrity of your official role and prestige of the international organization you work for," Pierre piled on her.

Collette stood up and fired back in a diatribe against her brother sitting on the opposite side of the table. "How dare you criticize me? It is none of your damn business to question how I live my life. I don't appreciate your lecturing me on morality, you should be lecturing your students on the immorality of the politicians who began the Nigerian civil war, and the economic implications for not just the innocent, poor citizens of Biafra, but the impact of the senseless war on the economies of Western Europe, too, Professor Pierre Durand," Collette remarked condescendingly.

"Hey! Hey! Cut it off, you two," interjected the eldest man in the house, Papa Durand. "First, I didn't expect this kind of behavior from both of you, especially in the presence of my two grand kids in our midst. And second, I didn't expect the topic that triggered this inappropriate behavior, either," said the senior Durand, turning to Collette, and added, "This is something you should have discussed with your mom and me in private first, instead of doing it the way you just did."

MRS. DURAND, COLLETTE'S MOM took her younger daughter by the hand and went upstairs to the bedroom she'd be using during her stay. They had one-to-one talk, as mother and daughter. Collette then shared the full story with her mom, including her plans to find a way to bring Udochukwu Abara to France, which she disclosed could possibly mean her going back to Gabon and legally marry him, to augment his chances of getting a Visa to come to France. Her mom was sympathetic and receptive to the idea, and promised to help in any way she could. Later on, after her siblings had left and her dad briefed on the matter, his facial expression gave no glint of approval.

"That's your choice," he said blandly. The following morning, Collette Durand looked in the city phone directory for immigration attorneys. She found a few names and made contacts for consultation appointment. She visited three immigration attorneys as scheduled, and all three basically had the same information for her that said—

"If you are married to a French citizen, you can get what is called, the 'Marriage Long Stay Visa, known as Visa de Long Séjour (VLS).' The visa allows you to enter France and remain for as long as 3 months or more, including up to a maximum of a year." *So, living essentially continuously together as a couple for a year gets him a foot in the door to apply to become a French Citizen or National.*

Armed with the information, Collette Durand would

return to Gabon to have a court marriage with Udochukwu Abara. Later in the evening, she spoke with her best friend, Emily and shared the good news regarding the immigration information from the attorneys she consulted. She told her that her next move would be a return trip to Gabon for the express purpose to try and bring Abara to Paris with her. She also shared the news of her plan with her parents and sister, Marie, and deliberately kept her brother, Pierre out of the loop. Before the week was over, she'd go back to the elementary school where she and Emily met, to talk to the principal for a possible comeback, after she will have returned from Gabon with Abara. By that time, her vacation period would be over, and since she wouldn't be going back to Nigeria, she'd resign from her employment with the International Green Cross.

Meanwhile, things were looking good for Abara in Gabon. Durand had called the immigration boss two weeks after arriving in Paris, and had learned from him that Udochukwu was successful at the hearing before the immigration judge for his asylum request. The immigration boss added that *"The hearing took an intriguing turn that was quite dramatic, when the judge learned from the young man that his real name is Udochukwu Abara, and that he was captured as a Biafran soldier on the battle field and held in captivity in a military prison as a prisoner of war, where he had the good fortune of meeting you. The army uniform he wore with the rank of 2nd Lieutenant, and the name John Bode he was introduced as, were fake. He didn't go into any more details, and the judge essentially concluded that whatever he did to* *get himself out and into Gabon, was well worth the effort, and congratulated him. The real icing on the cake was that the judge said, the court would go ahead and grant him Gabon citizenship, under an exceptional provision in the law, since he's originally from Biafra, the new country that Gabon had recognized and was supporting. So he'd get a Gabonese Passport in his name. Under the exceptional immigration statute, he's automatically now on a fast track for a transition of status from being on asylum to being a naturalized citizen of Gabon within a couple of weeks. And that is not even all; in the interim, he was also granted a work permit, and a government agency is assisting him to find employment. I think we can say it all means a good 'Christmas Present' for him,"* the immigration boss explained.

That turned out to be extra good news to Collette Durand's ears. When she called and spoke with Udochukwu Abara, he was extremely pleased and so excited, confirming the string of favorable new developments, including most notably, his soon-to-be new status as a Gabonese citizen with a real Passport.

Chapter 18

AHEAD OF HER TRIP BACK TO GABON, Collette Durand met with her elder sister, Marie, who's a nurse and briefed her on the itinerary, and the status of her pregnancy still in the first trimester, with no baby bump showing just yet. She told her sister she's fully informed about the requirements to procure a Visa for Udochukwu Abara to come to France, and that she'd learned he had in fact, been granted asylum in Gabon, and is also on a fast track to be granted Gabonese citizenship.

Slowly, Collette's father, after a while, came to terms with his daughter's decision and became more accommodating of her plans. He and his wife, had some talk with their son, Pierre Durand, the economics professor, to straighten things out and mend fences between the two adult children, following the row they had during the family dinner in honor of Collette's return from Nigeria. Pierre called Collette and apologized for his insensitive remarks. Collette accepted his show of remorse. The cordial relations and spirit of family bond noticed during Christmas Day dinner at the Durand's home, appeared to show all family members were now in harmony and fully supported Collette. On the eve of Christmas, Collette Durand had called the immigration boss and Udochukwu Abara, respectively to say, "Merry Christmas!"

During her conversation with the immigration boss, she finally disclosed to him her relationship with Udochukwu Abara, and the plan for marriage in the offing. "Oh, really. Congratulations!" he said. "I'd always suspected there was something of a much serious connection between both of you."

"Yeah, I know," said Collette. "Now, I need a favor from you," she began—

"What is it?"

"I'd like you, if you don't mind, to stand as a witness for us at the court marriage in Gabon."

"I'd be pleased and honored to do that for you. Or, I'll instruct my driver, whom you'd become quite familiar with, to do so for you. Is that okay?"

"Oh, either way, that will be fine. Thank you so very much, Merci, merci beaucoup!"

"When do you plan to get married?" he asked. "After the new year, January 23, 1969."

"Okay, I'll save the date. Let me know when you arrive."

"I certainly will."

When she spoke with Abara, she told him to expect her back in Gabon around the beginning of the New Year. She did not mention a date specifically, but only said, something precious soon to happen.

As part of what she'd alluded to as '….precious soon to happen,' related to her Christmas shopping list of things to buy, which included a nice gray suit, white shirt and tie, and a pair of black shoes with a pair of socks for Udochukwu Abara. He'll wear the outfits for their court wedding in Gabon. She also got a gift pack of 3 ties, and a men's wallet for the immigration boss and his driver, respectively.

JANUARY 18, 1969—

COLLETTE DURAND HAD PROCURED the necessary documents she'd present at the French Embassy in Libreville, Gabon to support the travel Visa application for Udochukwu Abara. They included her bank statements, evidence of employment (International Green Cross – still current), and place of residence in France. Marriage License will follow after the court wedding in Gabon. This time, it was her best friend Emily, who dropped her off at the airport. Meanwhile, back in Gabon, a Ghanaian female immigrant, 24, single, working in the housekeeping department in the hostel-like temporary housing accommodation where Udochukwu Abara was staying, took interest in him during the first week of his arrival. She started making unsolicited visits to his room in the guise of coming to pick up Udochukwu's laundry to wash.

"Are you married?" she asked Abara during one of her visits to his room. The overtures would get intense and suggestive of something amorous.

"No, I am not, but—"

"But what?" she pressed him. "Tell me now, why are you hedging?" she said, playfully.

Udochukwu Abara seemed to be enjoying her flirtatious behavior, not realizing how risky it was, given what a whole new world of good fortune that had come his way being in a serious relationship with Collette Durand. *Être un bon garçon,*

"Be a good boy," Collette Durand had jokingly

entreated him before she left and flew back to Paris.

As was the case in some of the capitals in Western Europe, where opposing groups of African students engaged each other polemically over the Nigeria-Biafra civil war; Collette Durand witnessed that dynamic at play, when she walked into Paris Nord International Airport. One group of Igbo students, representing the Biafra side of the civil war, and the opposing group of Yoruba and Hausa students, representing the Nigeria side, respectively were embroiled in heated verbal exchanges. "Your leader should be arrested and prosecuted for war crimes in the World Court at *The Hague* for carrying out a war of genocide against Biafra," ranted the Igbo group.

"It is your leader, whose over bloated ego and arrogance, recklessly brought the war upon your people. He should be the one to face trial for war crimes," lambasted the opposing group from western and northern regions of Nigeria. "See now, you can't even go home to your Igbo land because of the irrational decision to secede, but we can travel to our land!"

Collette Durand could not stand the unsettling sight of the two groups engaged in a nasty episode of verbal altercation as proxies for the two sides of the real civil war still happening on the west coast of Africa, claiming thousands of innocent lives. As she made her way to Air France check-in counter for her flight to Gabon, it reminded her of how the war seemed to be getting very little global attention, ostensibly due to the political and civil unrests going on in America. Not long after she was checked in, came the boarding announcement for Air France

Flight G211 for departure to Libreville, Gabon. The Friday night flight was smooth, and arrival in Gabon Saturday morning was right on schedule. She had decided to take a cab to the hotel where she'd made a reservation two days earlier while in Paris. After she checked into the hotel, she decided to rest for a few hours before going to see Udochukwu Abara at the government funded housing, unannounced.

The Ghanaian female housekeeping staff's flirtatious behavior toward Udochukwu Abara had become so out-of-control that she was intentionally wearing skimpy clothes and exposing her cleavage when she came to Abara's room to pick up bed sheets and his clothing for laundry. She'd come to Abara's room at noon to pick up items for laundry, and started flirting with him in a sexually provocative manner after closing the door behind her and bolting the lock.

"Come on, are you not a man? What's holding you back? You from Ghana? Don't you like seeing me?" she said, as she leaned in and placed her hand on his chest.

Abara gave her a simpering smile as she started to caress him. His indecisiveness seemed to suggest he was enjoying her flirtatious behavior and playing along, thus encouraging her. But, when she started going down south lower to his groin with her hand, Udochukwu then realized she was going too far, and it was risky to allow that to continue. What if Collette Durand showed up unannounced? he thought. "No, you can't do this, you must stop!" said Udochukwu sternly pushing her away from him. She got pissed off by Udochukwu's physical reaction repelling her unwanted sexual advances, and kicked him in the groin, sending him staggering backward as he fell to the floor. "Okay, since you don't want me, that's what you get, you fool!" she said, sounding frustrated and stumbled out of the room.

Abara got up from the floor and closed the door behind her. And just seconds after she left, there was a knock on the door. He opened the door, and Collette Durand was standing right there in front of him.

"Surprise! Surprise!" said Collette, as she spread her arms wide open and gave him a bear hug.

Udochukwu responded with the longest two words he'd ever said, "Thaaaaaank God!"

"Look at you, so happy, looking a little chubby now, hah!" she said, adding, "And thank God for what, if I may ask?"

"Well, thank God to see you again, safely, Madam."

"Oh, yeah! Me, too," said Durand. "And by the way; will you stop calling me Madam, for Christ's sake?"

"I know you mean well, I suppose doing it out of deference given the age difference between us. But, when it comes to love, age does not matter. Don't be timid. I want you to feel free and get used to calling me by my first name. I am not your Madam, I am your *ta femme* and soon to be your lawfully wedded wife," Durand declared with unbridled clarity. She plopped on the bed, making herself comfortable. Abara sitting on the chair facing her, became emotional and teary eyed.

"Come, come…come my love and sit with me on the bed," said Durand.

Abara moved and sat next to her. Peering deep into

each other's eyes, Abara said to her, for the first time: "I LOVE YOU, COLLETTE."

They cuddled and kissed. Abara was getting all worked up and felt the urge to—

"Don't worry, my love. We got tonight, together in my hotel room, as soon-to-be husband and wife," Durand promised.

Abara asked about her trip back to France, how things went at home, and inquired after her family.

"They were all fine, thank you for asking," said Collette.

It was getting late in the evening.

"You will not be sleeping here tonight. We'll go back to my hotel room in town, and we'll talk about the things we're going to do next," said Durand.

Shortly afterwards, Abara packed his belongings into his suitcase, they got out, he locked the room, and they came downstairs. As they were exiting the premises, the Ghanaian female staff, who had a crush on Abara, saw them and gave him a contemptuous stare. Abara, again in his mind, said, *Thank God* Durand did not knock on the door while the Ghanaian lady was with him in the room behind closed door. He wondered what could have happened. How the optics of the situation would have damaged his lovely relationship with the God-sent French lady, Collette Durand.

They flagged down a cab, which took them to Durand's hotel. Udochukwu Abara's world was dramatically changing. Not only had he escaped from the dungeon of captivity in Nigeria as a prisoner of war, he'd been granted asylum in Gabon and subsequently had become a naturalized citizen of

Gabon in a short span of time, and is scheduled for an entry level job interview with *'Le Gabon City Transport Corporation in February,'* all thanks to Collette Durand, working for the International Green Cross, when they met in a military prison in Calabar, Nigeria. How that meeting serendipitously led to the unfolding chain of events seemingly defining his destiny, was something he could not fully comprehend.

After they ate dinner in the hotel's dining room downstairs and rode the elevator back to Durand's room, it was time to unfold the agenda for the next set of actions in line with her objective of returning to Gabon.

"I had come back to Gabon for us to have a court marriage that would enable you to get a travel Visa to come to France with me, legally," said Durand.

"The French Embassy would require our marriage license and supporting documents from me as your spouse for the visa application," she explained. Then she opened her suitcase and brought out the clothing she'd bought for Abara – the gray suit, white shirt, tie, black belt, pair of black socks and shoes to match – all laid out on the bed. She saved the best for last, and it was inarguably a seminal moment in their growing relationship that had a magnificent feel, with a depth of history to it. She brought out a small purple box, and opened it to reveal its content—

The wedding ring she wore on the day she was married to her late husband, and the corresponding ring of her late husband, which he was wearing the day he tragically died in a motor accident. She had saved both rings.

"I will wear mine, and you will wear his as yours, for our court marriage on Wednesday," said Durand, choking back tears.

Abara was overwhelmed by emotions, as he reflected on the great lengths Collette Durand had gone to demonstrate her love for him. "Here, put them on and let's see how they fit," Collette gleefully asked.

He put on the outfits, and they looked just exactly right, as if tailor made for him. As the night wore on, Collette went and took her shower, and then slipped into a comfortable, silky red nightgown. She put her curly blond hair down, and dabbed a refreshing fragrance at the back of her neck. Udochukwu Abara noticed how beautiful and cozy she was looking as she got into bed and curled up under the covers. He shook his head in disbelief and counted his blessings. After taking his own shower, he put on a pair of comfortable silky blue pajamas that Collette had also bought for him. And for the first time, since they furtively had the affair that was analogous to a one-night-stand in her office back in the military prison in Calabar, Nigeria – they were having a full night of sleeping together in the privacy of a nice and comfortable hotel room – totally relaxed in each other's arms with peace of mind.

Chapter 19

BY LATE SUNDAY AFTERNOON, Collette Durand called the immigration boss to let him know she was in town. When he picked up the phone, the noise in the background suggested he was in the midst of a company.

"Oh, Madam, welcome back," he said. "I hope you had a nice trip; I'm having some visitors in my house at the moment. So we'll see you at the office on Monday."

Collette, who all along had deliberately not asked him, but assumed he was married and living with his family, understood he was being cryptic and formal on the phone for obvious reasons.

Overwhelmed by emotions the day before as Udochukwu was leaving with Collette to her hotel room, he had forgotten his wallet containing his new set of personal identification documents – asylum and work permit, including some welfare allowance money – in the closet. He told Collette he needed to go back and pick up the wallet before someone gained access to it in the room. She gave him money to take a cab from the hotel to the place and back. Abara flagged down a taxi in front of the hotel and rode to the public housing location. As he walked up the stairs to his room, the Ghanaian female housekeeping staff saw him, and followed from behind in the hallway.

"So just because of the White woman you were with, you treated me like I was nobody," she grumbled. "Is she your mother or what? That's what is wrong with you African men, once they see White women, they have no regard for their Black women," she added scornfully.

Abara ignored her, and when she persisted, attempting to get into his room as he was opening the door, he threatened to report her to the housekeeping supervisor. The threat caused her to back off. He went into the room, found his wallet and picked it up. After making sure the contents were all intact, he pocketed the wallet, locked back the door and was out of the building. He caught a cab, and rode back to the hotel.

"It didn't take you long at all; did you find the wallet, darling?" said Collette.

"Oh, yes, Collette. Thank God!" Udochukwu said.

Collette was now happy hearing Udochukwu getting comfortable calling her by her first name, and not '*Madam.*'

"Oh, I forgot to tell you; I was also scheduled for a job interview at Le Gabon City Transport Corporation coming up first week of February. I'm told it's an entry level position in the accounts department," said Abara.

"That's wonderful news! But you may not need it or even attend the interview, if things work out well and you get the visa at the French Embassy this week. After our court marriage on Wednesday and we obtain the marriage certificate, we'll go to the French Embassy on Thursday. Assuming you get the visa, which I'm confident you will, on our way back, we'll stop by a French Cuisine I found out in town and have lunch before heading back to the hotel, and I'll make our flight reservation on Air France to Paris leaving on Saturday. It would mark the beginning of a new life for you in France, and a new chapter in our lives together as a couple with our baby on the way."

Around 10:00 a.m. on Monday, Collette Durand called the immigration boss. She told him they'd go to the municipal court for the marriage on Wednesday. He told her he won't be able to come, but will send his driver to stand in as witness for her. The driver, he said, will take them to the courthouse, and he'd instructed him to dress appropriately in a civilian attire for the occasion.

"Again, thank you very much," said Durand. "No problem, and congratulations to you and your fiancé."

"Oh, one more thing…." Collette said to Udochukwu. "Let's find out from the male staff downstairs at the reception desk, where you can get a haircut in town."

After lunch, they stopped by the reception desk and asked the staff on duty about a barber's shop close by. Sure enough, there was one located in a mall a few blocks from the hotel that's a walking distance.

"You want to go now, or later?" Collette asked Udochukwu.

"Now is fine," he said.

She led him to the front of the hotel, and away from the sight of the staff at the reception desk, she slipped some cash into his hands for the haircut. She went back up to their hotel room, and Udochukwu walked the few blocks to the barber's shop. He took a seat and waited for his turn. Against the soft background music playing on radio, the barber, a middle aged, dark skinned Gabonese man was discussing the ongoing Nigeria-Biafra Civil War with a few other patrons in the barber's shop. The man brought up the story he'd read in a British newspaper, *London Evening News,* about the mysterious escape of a captured young Biafran soldier *prisoner of war* from a military prison in Calabar, Nigeria. Unknown to them, the fugitive alluded to as the central figure in the Nigerian news story was sitting right there in their midst in the barber's shop. Udochukwu feigned ignorance and simply listened. After about 30 minutes, it was his turn to get a haircut. The barber asked him to select which hair style he wanted from a set of men's haircut photo samples hanging on the wall.

"Just a simple haircut, well-trimmed and looking nice," he said.

"Okay, I understand," the barber said, and proceeded to give him a nice haircut.

In about 20 minutes, the barber was done. Abara paid him and left. He was back in the hotel a short time afterwards.

"You look nice, darling," complimented Collette. "Simple and well-trimmed."

Udochukwu acknowledged the compliment, and added, "Something rather startling happened while I was in the barber's shop waiting for my turn."

"What happened darling?"

"A handful of men in the barber's shop, Gabonese I presume, were conversing in English on current affairs, and one of them shared a news story he had read in a British tabloid about the mysterious escape of a captured Biafran soldier prisoner of war from a military prison in Calabar, Nigeria."

"Oh, my God!" exclaimed Collette. "Darling, they obviously didn't know you were the prisoner of war escapee at the center of the newspaper story right there in front of them. I hope you didn't say anything."

"I did not. I simply listened," said Udochukwu.

THE SOON-TO-BE NEW COUPLE had gotten up early on Wednesday morning to get prepared. Collette Durand had her blond hair beautifully coiffed. She was dressed up in simple, white, sleeveless wedding attire that had a touch of elegance to it, and was wearing white high heels. Her makeup was simple and nice, and showed her to be a woman of exquisite taste and beauty. Her man, Udochukwu Abara, who had put on a little bit of weight, was looking sharp in a grey suit with a matching white shirt and tie, and black shoes.

9:30 a.m., the driver from the immigration boss arrived as promised, and was met in the lobby by the bride and groom, carrying a decorated Christmas bag containing the gift items for the immigration boss and the driver. Collette hugged the driver, and Udochukwu shook hands with him. After exchanging pleasantries, the driver led them to his boss's 4-door French luxury automobile Citroën he parked in front of the hotel. They got in, and he drove off to the municipal courthouse on Tambo Road, in Libreville. They arrived just in time for the 11:00 a.m. wedding appointment. After paying for the marriage certificate fees downstairs at the customer service counter in the building, they went upstairs to the nuptial room on the second floor, where the court clerk was. The driver stood in as witness while the officiating court clerk had Collette and Udochukwu place their hands on a bible to exchange the traditional wedding vow, *"...for better or for worse, and until death do us part."*

After that, with their marriage now consummated, the couple kissed each other to seal their vows. In the courthouse, a dozen commercial photographers were available to render their services. One of them, whom Collette had paid to take photos of their wedding ceremony, captured the event with Collette's camera and a Polaroid camera for instant color print.

Once they were done, Collette picked up their marriage certificate from customer service office downstairs, and they left. At Collette's request, the driver took them to a nice restaurant in the city, where they had lunch, served with wine, and they clinked their glasses, saying "cheers" as a toast to the newly wed. When they arrived back at the hotel, Collette and Udochukwu thanked the driver and handed him the bag of gift packages for him and his boss, the assistant director of immigration services.

"Oh, one more thing, Collette feeling a little tipsy, said to the driver; if you don't mind, I'd like you to take a picture of me and my husband in a different outfit." "I don't mind at all," the driver obliged. "Okay, give us a few minutes, we'll go up and be back shortly," said Collette. As she and Udochukwu rode the elevator up to their hotel room, she said, "Darling I like you to put on the army officer uniform you wore in disguise, when we left the military prison in Calabar, Nigeria for the photograph the driver will take of two of us. It will be a historic photo for remembrance." So Udochukwu quickly undressed, and put on the army officer uniform. "Darling, also bring with you the key to the room at the public housing so we can ask the driver to drop it off for us on his way back." Udochukwu grabbed the key and they rode back downstairs. The driver used Collette's camera and took a photograph of the newlywed at a remote corner behind the hotel. When they got back to the front of the hotel, Collette asked the driver for one more favor. "If you don't mind, please help us return the key to the room my husband was staying in at the public housing on Grandville Road on your way back, since he will not be staying there anymore," she said.

"No problem, Madam," said the driver as Mr. Abara reached into the pocket of his trouser, retrieved the key and handed it to him.

Upon getting into their hotel room, they plopped on the bed, cuddled and kissed. One significant page, in the new chapter of their lives together, had just been completed. ***"Voila! Fait accompli,"*** said Collette, beaming with delight.

UNDERNEATH THE LAYER OF JOY AND HAPPINESS of the emerging new dimension to Udochukwu Abara's life, was a lingering pain that was starting to bubble up to the surface. The pain stemming from the reality of not knowing the fate of his family and loved ones back home at his native home village of Afara, Umuahia Ibeku, in Biafra amid the ongoing civil war. In the quiet recesses of his mind, he recalled how, in the immediate aftermath of his capture on the battlefield at Abak, South East of Nigeria, the thought of survival had taken precedence over every other thing and repressed any thought or concern about his family, friends or anyone else back home. So with the dramatic, tidal wave of change in his life with a promising future, he was beginning to feel the absence of his birth family. He needed to share with them the news of his good fortune. The mood swing did not go unnoticed.

Collette Durand, now Mrs. Collette Abara, took notice of her husband's emotional situation, and was genuinely concerned. They both wrestled with the severity of impaired communications system in Biafra and the inability of its citizens to communicate with relatives abroad. On the Nigerian side of the civil war, things were a whole lot different by comparison. Soldiers at the war fronts kept in touch with their families and loved ones through the country's telecommunication and postal service system. There was nothing like economic blockade wreaking havoc on the lives of citizens. In Lagos, Kaduna, Jos, Ibadan, Calabar, the rhythm of daily life continued to flow without interruption. Schools were open, people went about their businesses, and travelled to destinations around the country relatively with ease. But not so in Biafra. There was no way of readily knowing the situation with the family of Udochukwu Abara back home.

"CHEER UP MY LOVE, everything will be fine," said Mrs. Collette Abara, trying to lift up Mr. Abara's spirits, while he was pensively staring at the ceiling as they lay in bed side by side.

After dinner, Mrs. Abara assembled the documents that would be required for Mr. Abara's travel visa application at the French Embassy. Before bedtime, she called her sister to let her know that they'd been married at the courthouse in Gabon, and would be going to the French Embassy the next day for the visa application.

"Congratulations!" said her sister. "I have rented the one bedroom apartment for you in Paris as we planned," she added.

"After we get the visa hopefully tomorrow, we leave for Paris on Saturday with Air France, departing Gabon at midnight and arrive Paris around noon," said Collette.

"Let me know when you arrive and I'll have the keys to the apartment when I come to pick you two up from the airport."

"Okay, merci beaucoup, Marie."

Thursday morning. On the heels of tying the knots, the newlywed went to the French Embassy, on Naperville Avenue. Udochukwu Abara was looking sharp, dressed in the grey suit he wore for the courthouse wedding. The attending Consular Officer at the French Embassy observed in Mr. Abara's visa application that he was originally from Biafra, but had become a naturalized citizen of Gabon.

"No problem with that," said the Consular Officer, going through the checklist of documents required.

After certifying that the requirements were met, the Officer stamped in Mr. Abara's Passport, *"Approuvè"* with the placement of a Visa sticker, and said: *bon voyage*. Visibly happy after they left the French Embassy, Mr. and Mrs. Abara took a cab to Air France office to book their flight reservation for Saturday. They will spend the rest of the day getting some rest, while savoring the string of successes they'd recorded so far, in the execution of Collette's curated plan that originated from the military prison in Calabar, Nigeria, a couple of months earlier. On getting back to the hotel, Mrs. Abara called the immigration boss and told him that everything, from the court wedding to the French Visa application, went well as planned.

"I cannot thank you enough," she said.

"Oh, no. Not at all. It has been my great pleasure, I am glad everything worked out well. Congratulations to both of you," said the immigration boss.

"We leave on Saturday night for Paris," said Mrs. Abara.

"And by the way," said the immigration boss, adding, "let me say thank you very much for the gifts my driver delivered. I hope you do come back to Gabon for a visit someday in future with your husband. Again, thank you, I wish two of you plenty of success in your new lives together, and have a safe trip back home to France."

"The immigration boss could not have been more magnanimous," Mrs. Collette Abara thought, as she reflected on everything he'd done for her and her husband, from the night they arrived at the airport in Gabon, from Calabar, Nigeria.

Chapter 20

UDOCHUKWU ABARA SAW WINTER'S SNOW for the first time in his life, and felt the flurries melting on his body after setting foot in the beautiful city of Paris, France, the capital of one of Western Europe's enduring symbols of freedom and democracy. Marie had brought winter jackets for the arriving couple from Africa. As all three headed toward the exit doors, they couldn't miss the sight of the two opposing protesting groups of international students – pro Biafra and pro Nigeria – who had been a fixture at the Paris Nord International Airport since the Nigeria-Biafra Civil War began. The pro Biafra group demonstrators, mostly students of Igbo origin, were chanting antiwar slogans in their native vernacular, condemning Nigeria's federal military government.

Udochukwu turned to his wife, Collette and said, "This is amazing! I understand what they're singing."

Collette nodded.

"It gives you a taste of what freedom of expression is like in a democratic society," she said.

Forty five minutes later, they arrived at the furnished one-bedroom apartment Marie had rented for her sister and her husband. Before driving to the airport, she'd done some grocery shopping and stocked the refrigerator in the apartment with foods the couple will need for the initial couple of days.

"Welcome to France," said Marie to her new brother-in-law, Udochukwu Abara.

"Thank you, Madam," said Abara.

"Oh, Lord. Here we go again," Collette quipped, with a quizzical expression on her face, alluding to Abara's use of the word *Madam*, referring to Marie.

While they munched on cheese, crackers and assorted nuts with red wine, Collette called her parents and informed them she'd arrived France with Udochukwu.

"Welcome home," said her mom.

And her dad chipped in, "Congratulations! We look forward to seeing you two soon."

After Marie left, Collette and Udochukwu were now alone in their apartment, comfortably relaxed sitting in the living room sofa. Udochukwu seemed to be in a trance, his eyes darting around the wall with beautiful portraits of eminent French figures and artworks.

"Make yourself comfortable in your new home," said Collette as she got up to go unpack their suitcases in the bedroom.

Collette had decided against getting rid of Udochukwu's POW uniform. She wanted to keep it as a personal item of history for remembrance. Udochukwu took a shower. Soon he was feeling the effect of jetlag, and succumbed to a long nap. He woke up in the middle of the night. It will take some time for his body to adjust to the biological clock in the new environment. In the items on Collette's 'To Do' list were four major priorities: *1. Inform her boss, Dr. Alan McCollom, an American from New*

York, who's Executive Director of International Green Cross in Geneva in charge of global affairs and assignments, about her impending resignation as she'll not be returning to her location of assignment in Nigeria at the end of her vacation period. 2. Meet with the principal of the old elementary school in Paris, where she'd initially worked as a teacher with her friend Emily, to seek reemployment after her resignation from the International Green Cross. 3. Contact Emily's husband to see about hooking Udochukwu up with a part-time job in the motel chain where he works as a general manager. 4. Get Udochukwu registered in a French language school for foreigners in Paris to learn how to communicate in French, oral and written.

DURING HER PHONE CALL to Dr. Alan McCollom, her boss in Geneva, Switzerland, as a follow-up to her formal letter of resignation, Dr. McCollom commended Collette Abara for her service in Nigeria, and noted that the International Green Cross humanitarian agency will miss her. He however, mentioned something of interest the agency in Geneva had received from Nigeria's Ministry of External Affairs regarding a captured Biafran soldier held as a prisoner of war in the military prison, where then Collette Durand had served. The aforementioned POW, Dr. McCollom noted, was said to be missing and highly suspected to have escaped from the military prison. Dr. McCollom also referenced foreign newspaper reports that said the alleged mysterious escape was an embarrassment for military authorities in the country and consequently resulted in the demotion and removal of the army colonel, who was the director of the military prison, including the deputy director, a Lieutenant Colonel. He stopped short of mentioning if the reports cited any reference to Collette as the staff of the International Green Cross with oversight responsibilities in the care of the alleged missing POW. Collette Abara feigned ignorance and coyly said nothing about the story.

"Anyway, I thought I'd share the news with you," said Dr. McCollom, adding, "All the best to you, and good luck in your new endeavors."

Collette Abara thanked him, *"Merci Beaucoup."*

The principal of *Elodie Elementary School,* in Paris was pleased to learn Collette Abara had previously taught 4th grade in the school and was interested in coming back. "I've heard good things about you from some of the staff who were your colleagues, including Emily, who I'm told is a close friend of yours with whom you were hired the same day."

"Thank you," Collette Abara acknowledged the principal's kind remarks.

Within a month, she was rehired at the elementary school as a full time teacher. As requested, Emily's husband got Udochukwu Abara a part time job in Central Supplies Department at one of the motels he oversees as a general manager. As supply inventory clerk, Abara was charged with keeping track of motel room supplies (toiletries, laundry materials, etc.), items with depletion rates that raised eyebrows in the housekeeping department of mostly immigrant employees. The job schedule allowed Abara to work from 4:00 p.m. to 8:00 p.m. after attending French language school from 8:00 a.m. to 2:00 p.m. The transition plan as prepared by Collette from Nigeria to France, seemingly was working out.

Marie, who was the first person in the Durand's family to meet Udochukwu Abara at the airport, had seemed pleased and welcoming, Collette thought. But the gnawing question at the bottom of her stomach was how her parents and her brother, Pierre would receive Udochukwu Abara. The social temperature in the room when members of the family finally met Abara at the dinner in Collette's parent's house was low. She didn't need to be told her parents, especially her dad, had some reservations about her marriage, as was evidenced by the lukewarm reception, which nonverbally echoed their thoughts the rest of the time at the dinner. It was so awkward and painful for Collette watching her husband, Udochukwu looking so out of place and feeling uncomfortable. Other than Marie, who tried to engage Udochukwu with questions aimed at interesting the rest of the family about his country of origin, family background, and what have you; others looked vapid and disinterested. When Collette's elder brother spoke, the verbal interaction he had with Udochukwu was about his age.

"How old are you?" he asked dryly with a snooty attitude.

"I am 21 years old," said Abara.

It was obvious there was a subtle fixation not only on the age disparity between Collette and Udochukwu, but also on their interracial marriage. It was in the sixties, racial tension was still very much prevalent in much of the western hemisphere, and the family felt they couldn't just ignore that sociocultural reality. They'd expected Collette, in getting married after the loss of her French husband, to have a spouse who was French, or at least one of European descent.

THE EMOTIONAL FALLOUT of the experience at the dinner was very telling. The dinner had ended on a cold note. Not much of the variety of French dishes on the dinner table was eaten. The dinner did not last long. Pierre had left early, followed by Marie. So did Collette and Udochukwu shortly after Marie left. Later at night during a phone conversation between both sisters, they discussed the sour taste that the awkward dinner had left in their mouths. Marie confided to Collette what their dad's thinking was, as quaint as it had seemed, she thought.

"Mom told me that dad had questioned if you were in the right frame of mind, when you decided to marry Udochukwu. That he strongly believed you made the decision on a whim, driven largely by sympathy, and devoid of any sense of reality about the long term implications for your family regarding the French society's public perception of the interracial marriage, and the issue of age disparity between you and Udochukwu, being a young black boy from Africa."

Marie's revelation to Collette, metaphorically felt like a stab wound in the back. It created not only an emotional barrier, but also a physical one, too. Collette decided at that moment not to go to her parent's home again with Udochukwu. Meanwhile, the poor young man himself, Udochukwu at the center of the senior Durand's prejudice and discontent, began to have his own concerns predicated on his perception of the unraveling emotional saga stemming from the intercultural morass. If not for the circumstances of the war, he thought; was that the kind of marital relationship with parents-in-laws he and his own parents would want to have? How would his parents react if they learned he was married to a white woman, and one much older than he? Nonetheless, he reminded himself that he ought to put things in perspective, and count his blessings, and worry instead about whether or not his parents were alive back in Africa, where the Nigeria-Biafra civil war was still going on.

Every day on French television evening news broadcast, there was news report on the roughly two-and-half-years-old civil war. Collette and Udochukwu made sure they watched for status updates on the war. No report, as at that point, had indicated that the Nigerian forces had advanced beyond Abak from the Ikot Ekpene axis to capture the communities of Ikwuano and ultimately Umuahia town. On the advice of Marie's husband, Collette contacted the office of the local elected official representing their district to see about the chances of getting any relevant information regarding authentic updates on the war through diplomatic channels in government. When contacted, the office of the elected local representative provided information that pretty much echoed status updates on the war they got from watching the evening news on French television news telecast. Nonetheless, the problem of not knowing definitively the actual condition of Udochukwu's parents and family members in their home village of

Afara Ibeku, Umuahia, remained a persistent source of distress. The only antidote to the emotional dilemma was to continue to be patient and hold out hope that sooner or later, the civil war would end.

COLLETTE ABARA'S BABY BUMP was now showing, and as her stomach got bigger, it drew strange stares from a next door neighbor in their apartment building, an old French lady living alone, who was curious about Collette's marital status.

"I don't see your husband. The only person I see is the young black man, who speaks with a thick African accent," said the nosey old lady one morning after she exchanged greetings with Collette in the hallway.

Offended by the strange and unbecoming remarks, Collette tartly responded, "I don't appreciate your inquiry. Who are you and what business is it of yours anyway?"

The old lady recoiled, and from that moment on, never uttered a word again to Collette.

Udochukwu was showing remarkable progress in his study of French language. The preliminary French language course he took in high school at Anglican Grammar School, Ibeku Umuahia before the outbreak of the civil war, had been helpful, as he built on the knowledge of basic elements of the language he'd acquired. After he'd worked part time for a short period at the motel job as supply inventory clerk, and established a good employee record, he applied for a technician trainee position at the Peugeot Automobile Manufacturing plant in Paris, a job opportunity that was advertised in French newspapers. Luckily he got the well-paying full time job, with better prospects and attractive employee benefits. Collette was now well adjusted to her old teaching job at the elementary school and doing fine. Life for the couple was going well as they looked forward to the arrival of their baby, which ultrasound imaging that was performed determined the gender to be male. He'll be named, as chosen by both would-be mom and dad, *Emmanuel Akachi Abara.* First name Emmanuel chosen by Collette, and middle name Akachi by Udochukwu. When asked, Udochukwu explained to Collette that Akachi, in Igbo means, *"The hand of God."* Collette sagely remarked that the choice of the middle name in light of its meaning in Igbo was spot on. She couldn't agree more.

OVER THE REMAINING months of winter, Udochukwu repeatedly asked his wife Collette to take him to her parent's house when it snowed so he could take care of the grueling task of shoveling snow for them. He had seen how home owners laboriously shoveled snow, and thought he could assist his wife's parents in that regard as the right thing for him to do. But Collette vehemently opposed the idea.

"I will not take you there," she'd said, noting the unsettling feeling they both had resulting from the unpleasant experience at the awkward dinner in her parent's home days after their arrival from Gabon. Collette recalled how that negative experience at the dinner had strained their relations with her parents, particularly her dad, about whom he learned through her sister, Marie that he'd made bigoted remarks predicated on her interracial marriage. The young African son-in-law made genuine offer in good faith to go over and help out the elder Durands with snow shoveling, including domestic chores, such as lawn mowing or handiwork in the house, but Collette implacably refused to let that happen. The gulf, too, had widened between Collette and her elder brother, Pierre, the economics professor at *Universitè Paris Citè* (Paris City University), over the issue of her interracial marriage.

Now in his fifth month of living in France, Udochukwu Abara had 7 months remaining before he could be eligible for French citizenship on the merits of living together continuously with his French spouse for at least a year. By that calculation, he'll have met the legal threshold to become eligible for naturalized French citizenship in early 1970. Meanwhile, he continued to do well in his current job as automotive technician trainee at the French auto giant, Peugeot Automobile Manufacturing plant in Paris. His French supervisor, a man in his mid-forties, is impressed with Abara's dexterity in auto mechanics and expressed interest to pursue a career in automotive engineering. Udochukwu would find out that as a staff of the Peugeot auto manufacturing company, he automatically qualified to purchase new or fairly used Peugeot car if he wanted, such as 403 or 404 sedan or station wagon from the plant's excess inventory at generous discount prices. Talk of good fortune coming one's way, and being in the right place at the right time. If only the Nigeria – Biafra civil war would end soon, he wished.

Chapter 21
PARIS HOSPITAL

"WHO ARE YOU?" YOU DON'T BELONG IN HERE," one of the doctors in the delivery room shouted at Udochukwu Abara as his wife Collette was going into labor. It was an ugly incident based on racial prejudice. Just in the nick of time, Marie was coming through the door when she saw Udochukwu being forcibly pushed out of the room.

"Oh, Lord," she said with a contorted facial expression. "What is wrong?" she asked the man wearing operating room scrubs with his hands on Udochukwu's chest pushing him out.

"This person doesn't belong here."

"He is the husband of my sister, the woman in labor," Marie crisply explained.

"What? Really?" said the man, adding condescendingly, "He didn't say so."

"I think you owe him an apology for such an unwarranted humiliation," said Marie.

The man said nothing and walked back into the delivery room. Marie and Udochukwu followed behind him. An exhausted Collette, profusely sweating, lifted her face and saw her sister and husband. Luckily she had regular contractions, and the length of time she was in labor was considered to be within the range of normal birth. Collette took one final push, and the baby came out, to the exhilaration of everyone around her in the delivery room. Udochukwu's eyes recorded the seminal moment of history, when his son was born at 9:48 p.m., on the 23rd of September, 1969 – a male child to be named — *Emmanuel Akachi Abara.* The attending physician clamped and cut the umbilical cord, and the assisting nurse gently scooped up the baby and placed him on Collette's chest momentarily. Collette sent the good news of the day to her parents through Marie, her elder sister. After two days of stay in the hospital, mom and newborn returned home to their apartment.

AUTUMN 1968

FOLLOWING HER TRANSFER FROM ORON, South East of Nigeria, Akudo's stay at Yaba Psychiatric Center in Lagos was short-lived. It was not an ideal setting given her dual diagnosis of pregnancy and acute stress disorder. Suddenly alone in the city of Lagos, where she'd never visited even before the war, she had no psychosocial support system that would be essential for her care. Vast majority of Igbo residents in Lagos, including people from her home town, had fled in droves back to the east in the months leading up to the outbreak of the civil war. Those who for various reasons had stayed behind in Lagos, were said to have gone into hiding ostensibly for their safety, as there were rumors alleging that anti Biafra sentiments fueled ethnic hostilities, resulting in brutal killings of Igbos after they were apprehended in public transportation, such as buses, rounded up and taken to unknown destinations. Nonetheless; conversely, there were also stories about untold number of good Samaritans among Nigerians, who showed compassion, sympathy and exemplified humanity at its very best, protecting, sheltering and caring for Igbos. Among such Nigerian good Samaritans were not only individuals, but also religious institutions, like churches which lived by the ethos of the Christian faith, "One body, One hope, One spirit, in Christ."

As luck would have it, Yaba Presbyterian Church was one such religious institution of faith. Rev. (Dr.) Joseph Akpakpan, senior pastor of Yaba Presbyterian Church, arranged to provide shelter and care for Akudo in a place for the needy called *Dorcas Mission Home*, under the auspices of the church, in the vicinity of Yaba, close to Igbobi General Hospital, where Akudo would be receiving prenatal care. The church, under the leadership of Rev. (Dr.) Akpakpan, a man from Abak, South East of Nigeria, and was educated in the United States at New York Theological Seminary, became a conduit of hope, meeting the spiritual and psychosocial support need for Akudo through the parishioners, while the war lasted. Rev. Akpakpan had returned home from the United States and became pastor of the Yaba Presbyterian Church two years before the civil war began. When he heard the story of Akudo described to him in chilling detail — how she ended up in Lagos from Abak, his home town at the Ikot Ekpene sector of the war, a tight bond ensued between Akudo and the pastor's family. Akudo became sort of like their adopted daughter.

On the instruction of the pastor, the staff at Dorcas Mission Home, as much as possible, prevented Akudo from watching news broadcast of the civil war on *Nigerian Television Authority (NTA), Lagos*, for fear that visual exposure to the grim spectacle of suffering Biafran citizens, looking malnourished and skeletal, especially children with sunken eyeballs and bloated stomachs, will heighten her anxiety about the unknown fate of her parents, and compound her post traumatic stress disorder, in addition to a potential high risk for miscarriage. Whenever she asked to watch the television set, the staff told her the TV wasn't working. Although Akudo was being accommodated in Dorcas Mission Home, a private housing for the needy funded by a religious organization, she was technically still under the custody of the Nigerian military. Nine months into her pregnancy, the size of her stomach clearly indicated delivery of her baby was imminent.

LAGOS HOSPITAL

IT WAS NOT HOW she had envisioned life to be for her, in the context of what would be happening soon in Igbobi General Hospital, Yaba, Lagos. Memory flashback from earlier times spent with her fiancé, Biafra Army Captain Obioma Okoro took center stage in her mind. She recalled the plan they had about getting married after Okoro will have graduated from University of Nigeria, Nsukka with a degree in architecture and landed a lucrative job. The dream she had of becoming pregnant with a male child during her visit to Captain Okoro's warfront location at

Abak, and with him being by her side to witness the birth of their baby she'd proposed to name, *Obiagha, "heart of war."* Against the backdrop of those sentiments, tears welled up in her eyes as she began to go into labor, and cried, "Obim… Obim… Obim, where are you, Obim?"

Mrs. Esther Akpakpan was in the delivery room to give her emotional support. She understood Akudo was having flashback of memories, crying out the name, "Obim…" in apparent reference to her fiancé, Capt. Obioma Okoro, presumed no longer alive.

"My daughter push, push…you hear me? It will be okay," said Mrs. Akpakpan. "Everything will be fine in Jesus name," she assured her.

After several hours of stalled contractions and prolonged labor, the attending OB/GYN physician was beginning to consider performing surgical delivery of Akudo's baby by *C-section.* Then suddenly, one more push with every fiber of her being, the baby came out of her to the warm cheers of everyone in the delivery room.

"Praaaaaise the Lord! Praise the Lord! Thank you Jesus! Thank you Jesus!—" Mrs. Akpakpan chanted with joy. *Obiagha Obioma Uwalaka* was born at 10:32 P.M., on 4th of July, 1969.

The Military Affairs Liaison Officer at Yaba Psychiatric Center, who periodically checked in on Akudo to see how she was doing, was officially notified that she'd successfully given birth to her baby, for update in her medical record.

Chapter 22
JANUARY 1970

DISPROPORTIONATELY OUTSIZED IN NUMERICAL STRENGTH, and outmatched in military assets; not many had thought Biafra would survive for as long as it did, once the first shot that began the war was fired by the Nigerian forces. The Nigerian federal troops had launched the initial attack from the Northern flank of the border between the then eastern region and the northern region of Nigeria. But the relatively small, secessionist nascent Biafra, stunned the world with its undaunted will to defend itself. The Nigerian side of the conflict had misjudged the resolve of the new country to fight back. And fight back it did. It tactically redistributed its military combat resources toward the Southwestern axis, and its army made ferocious incursions into the Midwest, gaining grounds advancing deeper into the Western region. That rapid advance dramatically came to a chilling halt, when skirmishes and betrayals in Biafra military leadership reportedly resulted in breakdown of combat confidence within the army. Top Biafra army officers were said to have sold out to Nigerian forces in egregious military intelligence sabotage. The Biafra self-inflicted military failure became the Achilles heel that led to rapid loses. Nigerian federal forces launched counteroffensive operations that pushed back the Biafran forces all the way across the River Niger to the mainland, Southeast. The retreat marked a paradigm shift in the dynamics of the conflict and altered the face of the war from then on. Nonetheless, back in Biafra's mainland, its fighting forces regrouped and regained the will to keep on fighting. The war lingered for the next two and half years and counting—

While it lasted, Biafra suffered battlefield defeats immensely in its military manpower, with the incremental loss in territorial control, as one city after another, fell like a pack of dominos, and the stifling economic blockade made its defeat inevitable. Umuahia and its communities were now the vestigial territory under the control of Biafra as the seat of the crumbling government. By mid-January 1970, a major offensive launched by the Nigerian forces from the Southeastern sector, would be decisive.

IN THE FINAL HOURS OF THE WAR, there was wild uproar and chaos as the fleeing villagers of Ikwuano communities drifted aimlessly on the road. Many took to the bush in the interior areas of the villages to look for a hiding place in the woods. A woman in Amawom village named Dorcas, in her early sixties --- like so many others caught in the precarity of the moment — had grabbed some of her belongings and fled with her only child, a boy, Ukachi, 15, to the interior outskirts of the village to take refuge in a valley called "Iyi Oson" with a stream flowing through it. Before they fled, she'd buried some of her valuable possessions: a Singer sewing machine and a large metal pan for frying mush cassava to produce dry gari, hoping to dig up and retrieve the items if they survived and returned home. As dusk settled, tension hung like a thick fog in the air over the villagers taking refuge in the valley. Dorcas and her son found a spot under a palm wine tree and lay down on a raffia mat. Her son had put on a blouse to disguise himself as a female. It was believed that enemy forces notoriously took Biafran males away to unknown destinations in places where they'd captured. As more of the villagers streamed into the valley, a pervasive sense of hopelessness took hold, with the evening of chaos ticking away by the minute. In what seemed like the people had reached the nadir of life, someone was heard barking an order demanding that children crying uncontrollably, and domestic animals bleating be summarily silenced, for fear that the noise would give away their hideaway location and increase the frightening prospect of the Nigerian troops finding them. The bizarre call to silence crying children showed just how hopeless and out of control the dire situation had become.

A dramatic scene ensued, involving two men who were embroiled in a heated argument over a bleating goat near where Dorcas and her son were lying. It was a frightening episode about to turn violent as tempers flared. Both men had weapons pointed at each other, their faces contorted with rage. One had a long machete wielding it in front of his opponent's face, and the other had a handgun he aimed at the other man's stomach. The machete wielding man in his fifties, was the older of the two men and owner of the bleating goat. His younger opponent was in his twenties, and was the one with the pistol. He was so irate that he was threatening to shoot and kill the bleating goat. "If you don't kill your goat right now, I'll kill it."

"Over my dead body would that happen," said the older man in defiance, wielding his machete. "I dare you to go ahead and shoot the goat and see if I'll not cut off your head right now in one fell swoop."

Dorcas and other adults nearby, frightened by the escalating tension threatening to turn into a bloodbath, rushed over to intervene. They pleaded to both men to call off the insanity and avert an incipient homicide. Both men, their bodies still trembling with rage adamantly stood their grounds, refusing to listen to the voices of reason trying to end the potentially deadly conflict. Dorcas decided to make a dramatic move. She threw herself right into the middle of both men.

"OK, since both of you are hell-bent on killing each other, you will have to kill me first," she grimly proposed hoping to challenge the conscience of both men and coerce them to drop their weapons.

Surprisingly that last minute stunt worked. It melted their hearts. The two men backed off from the gripping insanity that was the ugly spectacle people around had just witnessed. It was a watershed moment for Dorcas, whose courageous gambit for peace in the atmosphere of looming catastrophe in the valley, had paid off. She reminded both men of the heinous atrocity they had come dangerously close to committing — kinsmen killing each other — and the trail of deadly consequences that would've haunted both families for generations, according to widely held belief in the native culture of the land. The goat that sparked the conflict was eventually slaughtered by its owner, roasted and shared among the families hunkered down in the valley. Dorcas's son Ukachi took a bite, but it was tasteless, he had no appetite to eat the meat. They were still frightened and despondent, counting their days eerily contemplating what they perceived as their last hours on earth. Grim imagery of mass murder dominated everyone's psyche.

As the sound of automatic gunfire and exploding mortar got louder, it became clear that the Nigerian troops were getting closer to Amawom village or might even have arrived. Something had to be done urgently to prevent the enemy Nigerian troops from coming down to the valley and kill everyone. A group of men got together to brainstorm for ideas. They came up with an idea to send someone to go out and welcome the Nigerian troops and convince their commander that an entire group of frightened and displaced villagers were in the valley hoping and praying that their lives would be spared. The idea sounded great but the problem was getting someone brave enough to do it. After a protracted silence, with the men surveying each other's face for clues as to who'd volunteer, an elderly prominent leader in Amawom, volunteered to go as an emissary to save his people. He would go, armed with faith in God, hope and a white piece of cloth tied to the apex of a long stick as an improvised flag to wave at the approaching troops as a universal symbol of surrender and peace. Two other relatively younger men volunteered to accompany him. The two men would hide in the bush near the main road and observe from a safe distance how the mission would turnout and report back to the rest of the people hunkered down in the valley, holding their breaths.

THE IMPROVISED WHITE FLAG cut out of a white piece of cloth to serve as a symbol of surrender and peace was given to the elderly emissary to carry with him. After a brief prayer, the three brave men took off climbing the hill out of the valley toward the main village. The lead emissary made it out to the periphery of the village and emerged from the bush path opposite the Amawom Methodist Church. Now in open view, he was walking south along the shoulder of the road toward the adjoining village of Umugbalu holding up and waving the improvised white flag amid random shots being fired by the advancing Nigerian troops. Then suddenly, the dreaded happened. He was struck by a bullet, collapsed and died. Frightened by the horrible tragedy they'd just witnessed from the periphery of the road in their bush hideout, the other two men quickly retreated and made a mad dash back to the valley and relayed what had happened. "Our respected elder and brave emissary had just been killed by the road side near Amawom Methodist Church. Everybody, prepare for the worst," was the gloomy message from the two men that was passed around. It set off a tumultuous wave of anguish with loud screams and wailing down in the valley of *Iyi Oson* at Amawom in those harrowing, final hours of the Nigeria – Biafra Civil War.

An entire mass of people extremely distressed and expecting the worst, lay down in the valley frightened out of their wits going into the night. Then suddenly early in the morning the next day, some men in the village, with firsthand knowledge of what was happening following the arrival of the Nigerian forces, came rushing down the valley shouting, "The war is over! The war is over! Everyone can come out now."

It was a stunning announcement. Some people were elated and jumped for joy, others were understandably skeptical and still afraid. The brave ones who believed the news was real, began to climb back up heading toward the village. Later in the day, when news came back confirming it was real that the war indeed had ended, the skeptics who'd refused to leave, finally began to climb out of the valley and made their way to the village. The body of the fallen elderly hero emissary was subsequently retrieved for burial. Meanwhile, the vast majority of the locals ended up in the large facility of the Federal School of Agriculture, Umudike, a little over a mile away. It was designated as a holding camp, where they'd be processed as refugees eligible to receive assistance for their resettlement in their homes under a post war federal government aid program, which in reality, left much to be desired. Breathing a sigh of relief at long last, some young women among the families in the villages fell in love with some of the Nigerian troops stationed at Anglican Grammar School, Umuahia that was used as army garrison. Such families, whose daughters developed love relationships with the men of the Nigerian troops, became instant beneficiaries of relief materials in money and food items. Some of the love relationships cultivated in the immediate aftermath of the war, would morph into long term marital relationships.

THE NEW STATE

AKUDO'S BABY BOY WAS a little over 7 months old when the civil war ended. As the Nigerian Army under the auspices of the federal military government began in earnest the crucial task of releasing captured former Biafran soldiers and sending them back to their native homes, Akudo's case received quite an extraordinary treatment. With no known relatives in Lagos to contact and coordinate with, to facilitate her return back home to her family in the East, a decision was made by the higher ups in the office handling the task at the Defense Ministry in Lagos, to liaise with the office of the newly created East Central State under the leadership of a man named Ukpabi Asika, the State's Administrator. The office in Enugu, capital of East Central State, contacted the military liaison officer at the 3rd Division Nigerian Army Garrison in Umuahia to send some soldiers to Amawom village and find out who the parents of Akudo were, or members of her family, if they were alive to receive her upon her return. The objective was to make sure she was safely and properly returned home to her family with her new born child. Once word got back to the military liaison officer at Yaba Psychiatric Center confirming that Akudo's parents were alive, a date was set for her to be transported home to the East with her baby.

The government went to great lengths to mitigate any distressful travel condition for Akudo and her 7 months old baby. So travelling by road from Lagos to the East was ruled out, given the poor condition of the roads most of which were impassable as a result of the war. Arrangement was made to fly her with her baby on a Nigerian Air Force plane that made regular flights to Enugu on government business. The Friday before Akudo's travel date on Monday, 18TH of February, 1970, the military liaison officer at Yaba Psychiatric Center, met her at Dorcas Mission Home to present her with the paperwork of her official release from the custody of the federal military government. In addition, she received from the military liaison officer, the sum of *1000 Pounds* Nigerian currency as a gift, courtesy of the government, to help get her started on a new life following her release and return to her native home. Similarly, she received another pleasant surprise on the eve of her departure. Rev. (Dr.) Joseph Akpakpan, the pastor of Yaba Presbyterian Church, and his wife visited her after their Sunday church service. The kind reverend gentleman really proved himself to be a man of immense magnanimity. He presented to Akudo on behalf of the church, the sum of 500 Pounds, which members of the church had raised to bid her farewell.

"The door of the church is open, and the door of my house is open, too for you, should you decide to return to Lagos to finish your secondary school education," he said to her.

"We'll make sure you and your child are properly and adequately taken care of in my house or at Dorcas Mission Home, while you're attending school in Lagos," he added with a glint of hope and assurance in his eyes.

Tears of gratitude welled up in Akudo's eyes. She

began to sob, and dabbed her eyes with handkerchief.

"That's okay, everything will be fine, in Jesus name," said the pastor's wife, Mrs. Esther Akpakpan. And how lucky could someone be in the grand scheme of things; Akudo had lost one love in the heat of war, her fiancé, Capt. Obioma Okoro, and had gained another love of family in the support and grace of the pastor and his wife.

Chapter 23
ENUGU AIRPORT

STRONG STORM THREATENING a heavy rainfall was brewing when the Nigerian Air Force (NAF) Jet piloted by Flight Lieutenant Umaru Gambo began to make its descent on approach to landing at Enugu airport. The pilot navigated the plane through the stormy weather and landed it safely with his 4 – man crew of Air Force personnel on board, including Akudo and her child at around 10:45 A.M. They landed just before it started to rain heavily. On hand at the airport to receive her and her baby, was an army staff from the office of the Administrator, East Central State. Two other soldiers, armed with machine guns had come with the army staff.

After clearing arrival formalities, the soldiers took Akudo with her child and luggage to an army Land Rover parked in front of the airport. Even though the civil war had officially ended, the atmosphere was still volatile with lingering sentiments of bad vibes in the East. So the army didn't want to take any chances. It was still operating under military emergency mode in the East. It took extreme measures in providing armed military escort to guarantee that nothing untoward would happen during the road trip to Akudo's native home village of Amawom hundreds of miles away. The army Land Rover was well equipped mechanically to handle the hazardous road conditions from Enugu to Umuahia under the pouring rain. The driver made occasional stops at convenient locations during the long trip to allow for both mom and baby to feed and attend to the call of nature. At around six in the evening, they arrived Amawom. The rain had stopped, and there was still daylight. Amid the psychologically, painstaking task of trying to put their lives together, after a historical trauma of the three-year civil war, the Mbaru, Amawom Evening Market, known as *Ahia 4,'* had resumed, but not at prewar full capacity level. The market was beginning to wind down when the Land Rover reached the market square.

"Jesus Christ! Home again! Home Again!" gushed Akudo, on recognizing the familiar environment. The driver pulled over to the side of the road and stopped.

"Okay, can you direct us to your compound from here on?" he said to an exhilarated Akudo.

"It's a little further up the road," she said.

When the driver got to Mbakamanu, he turned left into a narrow dirt path that led to a sprawling sandy open space called *'Ama Mbakamanu'* and stopped. Akudo alighted from the vehicle carrying her baby. The soldiers did, too, looking friendly but very much on guard with their guns in full display before a small group of onlookers starting to form around the army vehicle.

ONE OF THE ONLOOKERS RECOGNIZED AKUDO and asked, "Is that Akudo?"

"Yes," answered Akudo.

To make assurance doubly sure, the young lady

further asked, "Akudo, the daughter of De Amos and Da Rebecca?"

"Yes! Please, go tell my parents to come out, I am home," Akudo said.

The young lady sprinted off to be the messenger of the epic news of the day. A mammoth crowd had gathered, some people with their hands clasped over their chests staring at Akudo in disbelief.

"Is this a dream or what?" one person asked.

Others broke out in cheers and chanted, "Thank you Jesus!"

"Jehova Jairo, thank you!"

Within minutes, the good news had spread around the village.

"Akudo. Is that not the girl, who left during the war to go visit with her boyfriend, the army officer from Umudike at Ikot Ikpene sector, and was never heard from again?" wondered one curious onlooker.

"Yes!" affirmed another. "Do you notice she has a baby with her? Wonder whose baby she's carrying," observed a third inquisitor.

"AKUDO! AKUDO!" AKUDO!" cried her mom when she and her husband finally came out and saw their daughter standing by the side of an army Land Rover with three soldiers next to her.

"Is this you, or my eyes are playing tricks on me?" she asked.

As dusk fell, the soldiers didn't want to waste time for histrionics. They introduced themselves to Akudo's parents and said they wanted to talk to them in private briefly before heading back to their base hundreds of miles away. The driver stepped away from the crowd with Akudo's parents to a quiet corner and explained their mission.

"God, almighty bless you and your colleagues," said Akudo's father. "Why not you and your colleagues come with us to my house for a few minutes and have some entertainment, at least kola nut or something, hah?" Akudo's father pressed.

"Oh, no. Thank you, Sir. I appreciate your kindness, but we have to go because we have a long way ahead. Thank you. God bless you and your wife," the driver said.

Then they walked back to the vehicle, and formally handed Akudo with her child over to her parents, thus completing their mission. They shook hands with both parents and bade goodbye. They would spend the night at the Nigerian Army garrison in Umuahia before heading back to Enugu the next day.

Early in the morning the next day, relatives and family friends began trickling in to see Akudo. As the day wore on, the visitors increased in number, with lots of questions on their lips. Akudo's maternal uncle from Amaya, who had a no nonsense attitude, took on the role as family spokesperson and told the curious visitors that Akudo was resting, and that the family needed time and space to emotionally reunite. But still, the visitors were itching to get the scoop, as one put it, *"on Akudo's resurrection."*

Akudo became the proverbial *'talk of the town.'* Upon her return, she'd asked about her best friend at OMEGRAMS, Comfort Uche, from Ndoro.

"She's okay," her mom had told her, adding, "We learned that she and her family survived the war, thank God."

"Oh, that's good news," Akudo remarked, and asked her mom to please find a way to let Comfort Uche know about her return. "I'll go to their place and inform her."

Over the next few days at night, in the absence of visitors, Akudo took time to share the story of her wartime odyssey with her parents. Her parents had lots of questions, and the foremost was about her baby, *Obiagha*. She narrated her story in riveting detail, starting from the Friday morning of the popular Ndoro market day she'd stepped out of their house and headed off to the war front to visit with her fiancé, Capt. Obioma Okoro, against the objection of her parents and many other people concerned about her safety. She told them how Capt. Okoro died, and how she came close to being killed herself, and ended up in Lagos, and gave birth to her child, whose father was her late fiancé. Her parents broke out crying. It was the first time in her adult life she recalled seeing her father cry.

AGAINST THE BACK DROP OF THE NEWS of Akudo's return, was the weighty issue of how to inform the elderly parents of Capt. Obioma Okoro that she'd returned home, and broke the sad news of their son's demise. Akudo's parents wrestled with how best to approach the task implicitly fraught with raw emotions. Being active members of the Amawom Methodist Church and well known to the pastor, Rev. Harrison Ironsi in the community; Akudo's parents solicited the pastor's advice on how best to handle the enormously sensitive situation. Rev. Ironsi came up with the idea to accompany Akudo's parents to visit with the parents of the late Capt. Obioma Okoro at their home in Umudike. On the Saturday Rev. Ironsi joined Akudo's parents to go to Umudike for the visit, cognizant of the high sentiments of bitterness sure to be unleashed, Akudo's best friend Comfort Uche from Ndoro arrived as her parents were about to leave. So while her parents were gone, Akudo with her baby, and her friend Comfort Uche were alone in the house, and felt comfortable without the intrusion of visitors, to reacquaint themselves with each other, after a long and traumatic three years of civil war.

"Girl, look at you, healthy, beautiful and a mom, I'll add," said Comfort giddily, as she took the baby boy from Akudo and cuddled him in her own arms.

"Comfort! Where do I even start? It is a long and complicated story that would make a book, my dear," said Akudo.

"But, main thing is, we thank God, we survived," she added, getting teary eyed.

"First of all, tell me about your fiancé, Capt. Obioma Okoro," Comfort squeezed in the question early on, her eyes lit with curiosity.

Akudo looked down, tears trickling down her cheeks, and said after a pause, "He was killed."

A brief moment of silence wistfully punctuated their conversation. "And this lovely baby?" asked Comfort.

"Our baby. Hmmm...." Akudo reflected, and then answered, trying to vividly narrate the scenario of events that transpired. "I took in the night I arrived at Abak, where he was stationed. It was the last night we slept together. As dawn was breaking, there was a surprise attack by the enemy Nigerian troops—"

"You will tell me more about the whole story, I am

sure there's quite a bit to unpack," interjected Comfort. "But for now, let me just say that God has a way with divine compensation. You lost Capt. Okoro, and gained his little baby boy," said Comfort, tenderly expressing her thoughts philosophically.

THE COLD RECEPTION

Rev. Harrison Ironsi and Akudo's parents were not under the illusion that their visit with the parents of the late Capt. Obioma Okoro would go well. Ironically, word about Akudo's return somehow had already leaked to the elderly parents of the deceased Biafran army captain. The reception Akudo's parents and Rev. Ironsi got from Pa Analaba Okoro and his wife was predictably chilly and fraught with anger. From the get go, soon as they were ushered into the living room of the Okoros, they were confronted with the inevitable question they'd anticipated, "Where's our son, Obioma Okoro?" Pa Analaba asked.

There was a momentary pause. "I am asking both of you, where is my son? Your daughter, Akudo had him killed, right?" he angrily doubled down on his question, literally accusing Akudo as an accomplice to the death of his son, Capt. Okoro. Akudo's parents cringed and took umbrage with Pa Analaba's incendiary baseless remarks suggesting their daughter was a murderer.

"But in all fairness, that's not true," rebutted Akudo's father.

"We wanted to let you know that Akudo would like to come and spend some time with you and your wife and share with both of you all she knows," said

Akudo's mom, in an attempt to calm down the distraught father of Capt. Okoro. "She also would like to come with the baby boy she and your son had," she added.

"What? Over my dead body!" Pa Analaba stormed, standing up angrily dismissing the proposition. "I do not want to see her foot in this house. I hold your daughter accountable for whatever had happened to my son."

As his emotions boiled over, his wife, Ma Agnes Okoro remained calm and pensive. Rev. Harrison Ironsi, interjected, and calmly said to the bereaved father, "Pa Analaba, your feelings are understandably normal and well appreciated in light of the circumstances under which the intensity of the pain you feel, and we all feel are being expressed. No one will deny that the loss of an illustrious and courageous son from this community, whom you and your wife had great expectations for in life, is not a devastating tragedy that leaves a huge hole in the heart. What I will say is that we will continue to pray for you and your family for God's healing grace and long-lasting comfort. For now, I think we will leave."

The vitriolic behavior Akudo's parents observed during their visit would become a major issue of safety concern for their daughter and her child. After a lengthy conversation with her parents, the tension would cause Akudo to revisit the offer Rev. (Dr.) Joseph Akpakpan, pastor of Yaba Presbyterian Church, who with his wife, Mrs. Esther Akpakpan, had made to her before she left Lagos.

"The door of the church is open, and the door of my house is open, too for you, should you decide to

return to Lagos to finish your secondary school education.... We'll make sure you and your baby are properly and adequately taken care of in my house or at Dorcas Mission Home, while you're attending school in Lagos."

Like so many other schools in the new East Central State, Oboro Methodist Grammar School, OMEGRAMS, renamed Oboro Secondary School by the new government, was getting ready to reopen. Comfort Uche had visited Akudo again at her place in Amawom, and both friends talked at length about resuming their secondary school education. Akudo shared with Comfort the unpleasant experience her parents had when they visited with her late fiancé's parents. "In blistering remarks, Capt. Obioma Okoro's dad accused me of being involved in the death of his son, and vehemently refused to even see me and my poor little baby I had with his son."

Akudo then added that the tension had impelled her to revisit the offer made to her by the minister in Lagos, Rev. (Dr.) Joseph Akpakpan, pastor of the Yaba Presbyterian Church, who was largely instrumental in the overall care she received, while the war lasted.

"So you wouldn't mind going to finish up your secondary education in Lagos," Comfort quipped.

"Are you kidding me? Of course, yes I wouldn't mind relocating to Lagos to finish up, for safety consideration. It would be wise to do so, given the tense atmosphere. You never can tell what a person may do when distraught and incredibly angry," said Akudo.

"Do you have a school in mind?" asked Comfort.

"No. When I get to Lagos, the pastor will help me decide which school, since his church will also be sponsoring me."

"Oh, yeah? Lucky you. Girl, I don't blame you. Bottom line is, do whatever is best for you and your child."

The insane and aggravating remarks of Pa Analaba, the bereaved dad of Capt. Obioma Okoro over the survival and return of Akudo without his son, leaked out in Amawom and Umudike villages. Public opinion on the old man's conspiracy theory that fueled his negative reaction was divided. While some people were understandably sympathetic and condoned the negative sentiments he subjectively spewed given the circumstance of his grief, others were sympathetic but condemned his vitriolic behavior in unjustifiably accusing Akudo of being complicit in the death of his son during the war. Akudo and her parents jointly agreed she'd relocate to Lagos to complete her secondary school education. They also decided to keep the move confidential. They'd be tightlipped whenever anyone asked about Akudo and her child, or seemed interested to know their whereabouts. Akudo sent a letter to Rev. (Dr.) Joseph Akpakpan, saying she'd decided to come back to Lagos in light of his offer, to finish her secondary school education. The pastor and his wife were so delighted and sent back a reply, saying they were happily looking forward to having her back in their home and in their church family. After the civil war ended, Akudo had been flown from Lagos on a Nigerian Air Force jet on her return trip to her native homeland. It had made her feel like a VIP, *very important person*. But she'd be returning to Lagos like a VOP, *very ordinary passenger* in the back wooden seat compartment of a commercial truck, *Chidi Ebere Transport Limited,* which was one of a few major mass transit operators to resume interstate transportation service to Lagos, Zaria, Kaduna, Kano and other major cities in the country. *Chidi Ebere, Ekene Dili Chukwu, Izu Chukwu, Inyang Ete,* and others like *The Young Shall Grow,* which later emerged on the scene of Nigeria's interstate mass transit operation, were commercial transportation legends of the road, whose services contributed immensely in fostering reintegration and uniting the country after the civil war.

After arriving Lagos, Akudo took an advanced placement examination for enrollment in Form 3. She passed the exam and was accepted into Wilson Memorial Girls Secondary School, Surulere, Lagos. She juggled the competing responsibilities of a young nursing mother and a full time high school student. Her status as a young mother was well guarded; it was never disclosed to the school. Ironically, her looks as a beautiful young lady with attractive feminine features, would make her physical appearance a problem of distraction for some of the male teachers in the school. Her chemistry teacher, Moses Olabisi, 34, a graduate of University of Lagos, and married man of two children, would get himself in trouble and lose his job, for making inappropriate sexual overtures to her. Olabisi had proposed to have sexual relations with Akudo in exchange for good grades in his chemistry class. When Akudo contacted the principal of the school, an investigation into the allegation of inappropriate sexual behavior was conducted, and it resulted in the dismissal of the chemistry teacher.

MEANWHILE, BACK HOME IN THE EAST at Oboro Secondary School, formerly Oboro Methodist Grammar School (OMEGRAMS), news about Akudo's capture during the civil war and eventual return back home, was the dominant topic of conversation among returning old students on campus, most of whom were her former classmates. She became sort of a high profile student others were anxious to see and learn more about her wartime odyssey; how she was captured at the war front, how she survived and ended up in a psychiatric hospital in Lagos, and finally returned home after the war. Even the pioneer Principal, Mr. H.C. Ogbonna, who knew her from when she started in Form 1 before the war, talked about her quite a bit during his welcome address to the students on the first day the school reopened.

The Principal noted that it was a rare blessing to have back in the community and soon in the school, Akudo Uwalaka, one of the returning old students who lived through the historic trauma of the civil war in extraordinary circumstances that were heavily challenging. But unknown to the principal, Akudo would not be returning to OMEGRAMS. She'd made an alternative choice to finish up her secondary school education in Lagos. After the Principal's speech, one student was overheard saying to another, "Too bad we're living in what is regarded as third world country. If this were a place like America or Britain, Akudo's personal true life story would be turned into a book with millions of copies sold, and potentially fetch her a lot of money."

For the two-year duration of her education at Wilson Memorial Girls Secondary School in Lagos, Akudo lived with the Rev. (Dr.) Joseph Akpakpan's family. They'd provided accommodation for Akudo and her child in the boy's quarter of the pastor's residence at Yaba Presbyterian Church, and she went to school as a day student using public transportation. The Presbyterian Church not only sponsored her education at Wilson Memorial Girls Secondary School by way of tuition, books and supplies; the Church also provided childcare for her baby in a nursery run by the church. The generous setup thanks to Rev. (Dr.) Akpakpan and the church was so conducive that it paid off for her handsomely. Akudo established herself as a bright student, earning high grades in all of her subjects in school, and ultimately in her final year, scored an impressive 'Grade One' result in her *West African School Certificate* examination in 1972. That paved the way for the receipt of a federal government scholarship, and her success in gaining admission to the University of Lagos, UNILAG to study microbiology.

While an undergraduate student at UNILAG, she met and fell in love with a young man in his late twenties, Dr. Davis Ekpo, a professor of architecture at the same university, who happened to be a member of the Yaba Presbyterian Church, and hailed from Rev. (Dr.) Akpakpan's home town of Abak, South East of Nigeria. After Akudo's graduation from

UNILAG in June of 1976 with a *First Class Honors (B.Sc.) degree in microbiology,* they tied the knots as husband and wife, in a spectacular wedding ceremony. The officiating minister, Rev. (Dr.) Joseph Akpakpan couldn't be more proud and enormously pleased.

"This is a union of divine destiny," he told a reporter of *Lagos Weekend* during an interview about the event, which was published in the newspaper.

ENFIN TERMINÉ! The news of the Nigeria Biafra civil war finally over was greeted with great cheers in France. Udochukwu Abara was taking his break in the staff lunch room, when his supervisor came in and gleefully showed him the headline news of the day on the front page of *Le Monde*. After a protracted, agonizing three-year civil war, the Nigeria-Biafra war was finally declared over on January 15, 1970, the newspaper said.

A few minutes later, he took a call from the automaker receptionist's office transferred to him for pick up on the phone extension in the staff lunch room. The caller on the other end of the line was his wife Collette.

"Have you heard the good news? The Nigeria-Biafra civil war is over. Finally over!" said Collette, citing French Television news broadcast report, including the BBC world news on radio, and a host of other foreign news outlets.

"Yes! I'd just seen the newspaper report on the front page of *Le Monde,*" Udochukwu said with excitement.

The timing was perfect. Not long before, he had officially become a French citizen having met the national eligibility requirement on account of living together with his French Citizen spouse continuously for at least a year. He couldn't wait to travel with his French passport to Nigeria with his wife and child to visit his native home village. His obsession with the prospective visit grew by the day. But first, he needed to find out if his parents and family members had survived the war. Postal and electronic communication services needed to be restored in the East. In addition, reconstruction of roads damaged during the war, became some of the top priorities of the federal military government to pursue reconciliation and foster reunification. Although the East was still reeling from the historic trauma of the civil war, the resilience of its people known for their ingenuity, enterprise and industry, saw them take on the initial challenges of rebuilding their lives and lands in earnest. Commercial transportation services sporadically sprung up in cities across the East Central State as one of the early forms of business enterprises to kick up the tempo of economic and social activities in the effort to return life to normalcy. British made Morris Minor and Peugeot 404 sedan commonly plied the roads as taxis within town limits. Peugeot 404 station wagon and Mercedes Benz 911 trucks and buses were the favorites for intercity and interstate long distance travels. Early pioneers of interstate commercial transportation services – *Chidi Ebere, Ekene Dili Chukwu, Izu Chukwu, and Inyang Ete buses* — reclaimed their spots in the commercial transit industry.

One of the remarkable developments in the immediate aftermath of the civil war, was the robust economic activities in Nigeria's petroleum industry.

Harnessing of the country's rich natural assets of fossil fuel accounted for the country's booming petroleum industry. The federal military government to its credit embarked on large scale public works projects that saw a boon in the construction industry. International giant construction firms, such as Germany's Julius Berger and others, were the recipients of mega contracts awarded by the government for highway network road and bridge construction projects transforming the landscape of the city of Lagos in the bid to curb the notorious traffic jam euphemistically called *go-slow*. The massive Keynesian economics modeled public works projects driving the national economy would become a major contributing factor in a significant migration shift in the country. The construction projects in Lagos drew people from the East just coming out of the civil war in droves. The economic benefits were observed back home in the East, as survivors of the civil war gainfully employed in the construction of roads and bridges in Lagos, remitted money to families at home, which aided in starting new businesses and enhanced economic renaissance in the East. Before long, the popular Igbo land cities of Onitsha and Aba, were pulsating again with economic energy as the commercial nerve centers in the south east.

POSTAL SERVICES RESUMED IN THE EAST. Udochukwu Abara sent a mail package addressed to his father c/o (care of) the Principal's office, Anglican Grammar School, Umuahia-Ibeku, his former high school, where he was a student before the outbreak of the civil war. The Principal's office had a clerk who did secretarial functions, and a messenger under the supervision of the clerk, who did local chores and ran errands outside the school premises. The messenger's duties included a daily chore of dropping off outgoing mails, and picking up incoming mails addressed to Anglican Grammar School, from the school's Post Office Box at the Umuahia General Post Office. The messenger had picked up Udochukwu's mail package sent from France, and was subsequently asked to go to Udochukwu's home village not too far from the high school, with a notification slip for his parents to come to the principal's office and collect a mail package from their son, Udochukwu Abara. At first, Udochukwu's father who received the slip thought the message was a prank and fumed at the messenger.

"Who are you and who sent you here to come and mock us?" he angrily asked with a disdainful expression on his face.

"I am from Anglican Grammar School, where I work. The principal's office clerk sent me," said the messenger."

"Well, I don't blame you or the person who sent you. Our son apparently died long time ago in active service as a Biafran soldier during the war."

"Oh, I'm sorry Sir about that; but it sounds confusing to me. The mail package for you to collect came from someone believed to be your son, according to the clerk," explained the messenger. Bemused, Udochukwu's father turned to his wife standing next to him, and with a stare of incredulity, uttered in their native Igbo dialect, "inukwa?" meaning "did you hear that?"

His wife said, "Well, I think we'll have to go to the school and find out."

Udochukwu's parents thanked the messenger and said they'd be at the school the next day to collect the mail package.

The next day, both parents went to Anglican Grammar School and collected the mail package that came in a courier envelope. It had the colorful markings around the edges of a typical mail from abroad, and the postage stamps depicting the iconic image of France's Eiffel Tower. On getting home, Udochukwu's father carefully opened the package as his mother looked on with bated breath. The content of the package shot a frisson of excitement across Udochukwu's father's face. Two color photos of Udochukwu, one of him alone, and the other taken with his wife and child; some amount of cash in French franc notes; and a letter stating he went to war as a Biafran soldier, and miraculously ended up in Paris, France. Full details to be shared when he visits home with his wife, the white French lady in the photo with his son on her laps.

"Are you saying this is Udochukwu, our son?" his mother asked in disbelief.

"I can see it looks every bit the Udochukwu we know as our son," replied his father. "He looks a little plumpy and have dense hair," he added.

Relief and reality seemingly began to sink in after Udochukwu's parents had gone to Standard Bank, Umuahia to exchange the French franc currency notes for Nigerian currency. To their pleasant surprise, the Nigerian equivalent was a whopping sum of one thousand Nigerian pounds, which was a good chunk of money for a family coming out of the civil war without any source of income. Soon, close relatives in the village learned about the news that Udochukwu Abara, presumed dead during the war, was reportedly now living in France. His parents showed visiting relatives the photos he had sent, of himself and his wife, the white French woman and their child together. Some 'Doubting Thomases' still weren't convinced.

"Only when we see him will we believe," one skeptic said.

Udochukwu's parents wrote back to their son confirming receipt of the mail package he sent to them with its content, the photos, the money and the letter. They added that there were some skeptics at home still not convinced about him being alive, since he'd long been presumed dead during the war. They asked him in the letter to make haste and come home so they'd all see him. Having become sure that his parents had survived the war and were alive; the assurance of restored postal service as a dependable means of mail delivery provided the impetus for yet another element of surprise he had for his parents. By December of 1970, Collette supported him with cash with which he purchased a white Peugeot 404 four-door vehicle from the Peugeot Automobile Manufacturing plant at staff discount price. They shipped the car to Nigeria as a joint Christmas gift from both of them for Udochukwu's parents. Udochukwu sent a mail package containing the documents of the car, including shipping, information, and a cashier's check for the estimated amount of money that would be needed to meet customs' clearance fees at Apapa Wharf, the major seaport in Lagos.

Luckily, things went as planned. Udochukwu's father waited for the estimated time of the shipment's arrival. Armed with the supporting documents received for the car, he traveled to Lagos in a *Chidi Ebere Transport Limited* bus, with a family friend, who drove taxi in Umuahia Township, and a male relative in his forties familiar with importation business. The latter's knowledge of goods importation business assisted considerably in finding a Clearing Agent in Lagos who took care of customs clearance at the Lagos seaport. They stayed in a motel in Apapa, Lagos close to the seaport for five days, with all expenses paid by Udochukwu's father, in addition to paying the two men with whom he traveled for their services. The taxi driver family friend drove them in the Peugeot 404 from Lagos to Umuahia. After the long drive from Lagos to Umuahia that started very early in the morning while it was still dark, and their arrival as nightfall was setting in, the driver pulled up in front of Udochukwu's parent's compound, and playfully honked the horn of the vehicle. It drew the attention of Udochukwu's mother and other members of the family. They rushed out to greet the men who had just arrived in the new Peugeot 404. "Praaaaaise the Lord!" Udochukwu's mother joyfully sang dragging out a note.

"Hallelujah!" the other members of the family enthusiastically responded in unison.

"I like you to come and see me tomorrow in the evening. I think my wife and I will like to offer you the chance to operate this car as a taxi in Umuahia town," Udochukwu's father told the driver. "It's a brand new car, as you can see. You stand a good chance of making good money for yourself and for us. Come tomorrow so we can talk and agree on the terms of the offer, if you decide to take the job," he added.

"Sir, this is fantastic! Glory be to God. This offer is God-sent, and I cannot thank you enough. I don't even need to think about it, I am willing to be your taxi driver. You will not regret it, I promise you. May God continue to bless you and your family," the driver went on and on expressing his gratitude and interest to be the driver of the prospective taxi.

Within a week, the car was duly registered as a commercial vehicle at the Umuahia Division of Motor Vehicle Commission. The new taxi driver began the job in earnest. He was delivering a given amount mutually agreed upon as a daily revenue, and whatever amount remained from the day's proceeds operating the taxi within a specified time period, was his to keep. He picked up the taxi at the owners' house Monday to Saturday, and returned it at close of business each work day. On the average, he made a lot of money for himself, sometimes as much as he delivered to the owners, other times, more than he delivered to the owners. Before long, life began to change for Udochukwu's family at home. Money deposits in the bank account his parents opened at Standard Bank, Umuahia, grew exponentially. His mother went from being a petty trader in Umuahia 'Ogumabiri' market to renting a big storefront in a prominent commercial zone in town, where she retailed numerous consumer goods in bulk, and became a wholesale distributor for Golden Breweries, the beer maker in Umuahia.

The family's enterprise in commerce was making remarkable progress, so much so that before long, two new storefronts had been added to their business. A storefront solely for wholesale beer and soft drinks distribution to retail shops, hotels and motels in and outside Umuahia Township. Udochukwu's father, whose job as *Track Maintenance Supervisor* for the Nigerian Railway Corporation, on the Umuahia-Port Harcourt rail line before the civil war began, and ended after the war, had been blessed with the good fortune that came his way thanks to the generosity of his son's wife, Collette, the French lady. He now ran the storefront that housed the inventory of wholesale beer and soft drinks to commercial outlets. The other new storefront addition, retailing consumer goods was now being managed by Udochukwu's elder sister, Oluchi. The Abara family's rising economic profile made them a fixture on the social scene in Umuahia. They became the-go-to family in their village whom many other families struggling economically approached for financial assistance such as trading land as collateral for loan. They kept Udochukwu abreast of how their lives had changed significantly for the better since the end of the war. Collette was pleased to learn about the good news of how things were turning out well for her husband's family, and looked forward to meeting them in the not distant future.

Chapter 25

"MAMA UDO," said Albert Abara, the pet name Udochukwu's father calls his wife, translated in Igbo *(Mother of Peace)*. "There's something I'd been thinking seriously about that I want to discuss with you," he began, when his wife sauntered into the living room and took a sit, looking half asleep.

It was almost midnight. "You see, since we received that letter from Udochukwu our son, saying he survived the war, and is now in "ala beke" (white man's land abroad), something had been bothering me about the picture of the white woman he enclosed in his letter, purported to be his wife. I am not happy at all. First of all, she is a white woman, and the other thing I don't like, is that she is a lot older than Udochukwu. That's not what I'd envisioned. My idea was that he would marry a girl from our land, younger, and a girl our family can control and mold into the kind of daughter-in-law we want her to be. Just think about it for a second, a white woman as his wife; how in the world is that going to work? How are we going to communicate and interact with her? How will our family, our relatives and family friends in the village understand or relate to her? From a cultural standpoint, it just doesn't make sense at all. I've been thinking of that young girl, in Obike

Ukandu family, who's in Form 4 at Holy Rosary Girls Secondary School, Umuahia. She'd be finishing up next year as I understand. I think I'll prefer her to be someone Udochukwu can marry."

"Eh, I hear what you're saying, but I don't think that is something to worry about at this time," said his wife as she began to articulate her thoughts in response. "The most important thing is to welcome our son and the white woman, and give thanks to God for sparing Udochukwu's life. Myself as the mother who gave birth to Udochukwu, I can't begin to describe how it felt when he voluntarily enlisted in the Biafra Army and went to war. I was afraid and worried for his life. Then all these years we did not see or hear from him during the war, I was heartbroken, living in pain thinking he'd been killed in the war. And then suddenly came the good news that he is alive and living abroad, something totally beyond our wildest imagination."

On a bright, Sunday afternoon, Albert Abara had done something absurd. Unbeknownst to his wife, he'd gone to Umu Achara compound to see Obike Ukandu and his wife, parents of the young woman, Ebere about whom he'd mentioned during the late night chat they had in their living room as his preference for Udochukwu as a wife. Collette he said, was much too old for his son, besides being a white woman, which he thought was culturally unacceptable.

"This unannounced visit to our place early this Saturday morning; anything wrong?" Obike Ukandu asked, as he ushered Albert Abara into his living room.

"No, nothing wrong. I simply came to discuss something very important you'd be pleased to hear," said Albert Abara. He cleared his throat, and then proceeded with what he had in mind. "You see, since my wife and I received the good news that our son, Udochukwu survived the war, and is now overseas, in white man's land; what we learned from him in his letter, especially the photo of the white woman he sent to us, had been bothering me. I am not happy at all. The white woman he said is his wife is much older, and the fact that she is a white woman is a problem for us and culturally unacceptable. So, I am thinking, I'll like to have your fine daughter as a wife for my son, Udochukwu."

Obike Ukandu let off a boisterous laugh that drew the attention of his wife.

"Good morning, Sir," she greeted Albert Abara, when she walked into the living room. "I said let me come in and see what was making my husband laugh so loud this early in the morning."

"I came to discuss with your husband the prospect of a potential marriage with your fine daughter for my son, Udochukwu, who as you may have heard, survived the war and is now overseas."

"Yeah, we heard about it. Oh, Glory be to God. Now, about our daughter Ebere; no wonder my husband laughed out so loud. Hmmm, your visit is well. In that case, I hope you two have a fruitful discussion on the matter. How's your wife doing? Please—"

Obike Ukandu cut in. "I can appreciate your thoughts regarding how you're feeling about the white lady. Any other parent in our land, being in your shoes would feel likewise. Well, all I can say for now, on behalf of my family, is that your expressed desire and interest in my daughter as a potential bride for your son, is a pleasant news. Nonetheless, you know our culture, customs and traditions, and the implicit protocol better than anyone else, to say the least. We shall be watching and waiting."

TRAVEL ARRANGEMENTS

HAVING PASSED EMPLOYMENT PROBATION and no longer a trainee, Udochukwu Abara was doing very well as an automotive technician with good prospects for upward mobility at his job in the Peugeot auto manufacturing firm. The good rapport he'd established with his bosses aided in the approval of his request for 6 weeks family vacation to Nigeria. He and his wife Collette fixed their vacation time to coincide with the start of Collette's elementary school workplace long summer break. Collette took the lead in making the necessary arrangements for their upcoming trip to Nigeria; applying for the Nigerian Visa for her family as required at the Embassy of Nigeria in Paris; booking their flight to Nigeria, and making reservation for hotel accommodation in Lagos. Udochukwu didn't have a Nigerian Passport yet; he'd be traveling as a foreigner with his French Passport.

Three months ahead of their trip, they'd jointly bought two other vehicles – Peugeot 404 Station Wagon and Peugeot 504 Saloon — from Udochukwu's workplace, the Peugeot auto manufacturer at staff discount prices. They shipped the vehicles to Lagos, and duly notified Udochukwu's father in a mail sent to him containing the vehicles' documents, which would be needed for customs' clearance at Apapa Wharf in Lagos. The Peugeot 404 Station Wagon would be an addition to the thriving commercial transportation business of the Abara family, and would be plying long distance routes, such as Umuahia to Aba or Port Harcourt. Udochukwu and his wife would use the 504 as a private vehicle to get around during their visit to Nigeria, and then either sell or leave it for his parent's private use at the expiration of their visit. Never in their wildest imagination did Udochukwu's parents think their lives would be so profoundly transformed economically in such a short period coming on the heels of a civil war thanks to the love, compassion and generosity of a French woman named Collette.

Collette had packages of gift items — clothing, shoes, handbags, wrist watches, jewelry — she'd bought to give to Udochukwu's parents and his siblings. She'd informed her friend, Emily and her elder sister, Marie months earlier about the planned trip to Nigeria, but had kept her parents out of the loop. On the advice of Marie, she called her parents to let them know she was traveling to Nigeria with Udochukwu for the summer vacation. She'd not spoken with her parents in a long time due to the strained relations they had stemming from her parents subtle disapproval of her interracial marriage to an African boy, Udochukwu, as he'd been pejoratively called, and whom her dad had tartly expressed was much too young, and had frowned upon the yawning age disparity between them.

"Okay," said her father when he answered the call. "Your mom and I wish you good luck on your trip to Africa."

The flight on Air France was smooth and landed at

Ikeja, Lagos international airport as scheduled. After they landed, Udochukwu seemed apprehensive and a little nervous as they approached the Immigration Checkpoint. He wondered if he'd been declared a fugitive, having escaped as a POW from the military prison in Calabar during the war. But his anxiety quickly dissipated on the assurance that the civil war was over, and he was coming in with a foreign passport anyway, as a legitimate citizen of France with his family. They went through Immigration and Customs formalities for arriving passengers without a hitch. Collette approached one of the flight attendants of the Air France they came on, a young, slender Caucasian French lady and asked for her assistance to pick a taxi to Federal Palace Hotel, Victoria Island, where she made reservation ahead of their trip.

"Oh, that's the hotel my crewmates and I are going to, too. We stay there whenever we fly to Lagos," said the Air France flight attendant.

She picked one of the airport taxi operators she and her crewmates rely on for Collette. The driver's appearance and accent, when he spoke, reminded Udochukwu of a traumatic scene he lived through in the dark history of the civil war.

"Welcome home Sir," prostrating, the driver said, in a thick Yoruba accent reminiscent of the voice Udochukwu heard on the battle field at Abak frontline, when he was captured by the enemy Nigerian soldier who aimed the barrel of his gun at him at point – blank range and ordered, *"If you move, I'll blow your brains out!"*

He gave the driver a mirthless smile as he climbed into the back seat of the British made *Hillman* Saloon after his wife and baby boy were in. Later in the evening in the hotel's sprawling dining room, Udochukwu and Collette bumped into the Air France flight attendant who'd helped them hours earlier get the airport taxi that brought them to the hotel.

"Don't forget to go to the French Embassy while you're visiting the country and let them know where you are," advised the flight attendant. "The French Embassy is located on the other side of the island on Ahmadu Bello Way, Falomo, Ikoyi. You can get the address from the hotel reception clerk at the front desk. While you're in a foreign territory, keeping the embassy informed is a prudent protocol, especially in the interest of your safety."

"Merci beaucoup. We'll certainly do that tomorrow morning," said Collette.

Monday morning after breakfast, Collette got the address of the French Embassy, and together with her husband and child, took a cab from the hotel to the embassy. The French embassy staff cordially welcomed them and duly registered their presence in the country in its *'Home Services Department'* as advised. While in the embassy, they took advantage of their telecommunications network system and sent a cable message to the Umuahia General Post Office via the Telecommunications Exchange Division for delivery to Udochukwu's parents. The cable message was delivered as a telegram at the address of Udochukwu's mom's storefront business location in Umuahia town. The telegram read—

"Dear mom and dad. We're now in Nigeria. Arrived Lagos yesterday. Call us at Federal Palace Hotel, Victoria Island tomorrow. Tel. 1 – 267 – 0472."

His parents received the message and called the next day from the Umuahia General Post Office, Telecommunications Exchange Division. It was quite an emotional phone call marked by the reunion of their voices after three years of separation by the civil war. Udochukwu told his parents that he and his wife with their little boy would need to stay in a hotel in Umuahia, nice and conducive enough particularly for his foreign wife during their visit at home. His father assured him that he'd arrange for a better alternative in a guest house in a more conducive environment at the Government Reserved Area (GRA) in Umuahia. The guest house, he said, is owned by Golden Breweries, a major company in Umuahia that had resumed production operations.

"I know the General Manager of Golden Breweries; his company supplies Goulder Beer to us as their wholesale distributor. We've cultivated a good relationship as close friends since I became the head of *Parents Teachers Association* of Anglican Grammar School. One of his son's is a student at the school just as your younger brother, Nkem. The Guest House was built as a suitable accommodation complete with modern amenities for German engineers who came to work on the breweries after the war and revived it for production operations."

"That would be awfully nice," said Udochukwu.

True to form, Udochukwu's father was able to leverage the influence of his social networking connection when he contacted Mr. Azubuike Elendu, the general manager of Golden Breweries to avail his son Udochukwu and his family of the company's guest house during their visit. The visiting couple and their baby boy from abroad took a Nigeria Airways local flight from Ikeja, Lagos to Enugu, East Central State. Udochukwu's dad had arrived at the Enugu airport. He had gone with a second driver he'd hired as a taxi driver operating the Peugeot 404 Station Wagon to pick up his son's luggage he was expecting to be a lot. He'd been accompanied by another driver who drove the 504 Saloon that was part of the latest shipment of additional vehicles Udochukwu and his wife, Collette had shipped ahead of their trip. He and his wife and child rode in the 504 from Enugu Airport to the Guest House in GRA, Umuahia, where they'd be staying during their visit, while his father rode in the 404 Station Wagon carrying their luggage.

Amid the joy of returning home to the land of his birth, was the somber reminder of defeat. All around the dry landscape as they drove through the towns in the East, Udochukwu and his wife couldn't help but notice the extensive tolls of the civil war, the ruins and remnants of dilapidated buildings riddled with bullet holes.

Chapter 26
THANKSGIVING AND RECEPTION

Udochukwu and his wife, Collette with their baby boy arrived Umuahia and were driven straight to the GRA section of the town, where they took occupation of the Guest House made available to them courtesy of the general manager of Golden Breweries. Collette liked the environment with the trees and gardens adorning the landscape, which gave the neighborhood an air of serenity. She particularly liked the spacious and comfortable accommodation. It made her feel very much at home. But there was something about her impression of Udochukwu's father upon meeting him at Enugu airport that didn't quite click with her. They'd hugged, but the reception she sensed seemed lukewarm. It was bereft of the kind of excitement she thought would be evident in his body language as her Nigerian father-in-law she was meeting for the first time. Instead, what she saw was a mirthless facial expression. It felt like an ominous sign of something lurking in the dark. She tucked that impression away in the back of her mind.

Over the weekend following their arrival, there was a 'Thanksgiving' service in St. Andrew's Anglican Church, Ahia Eke, Umuahia. The Thanksgiving component of the Sunday service program was at the behest of the Abara family in light of the survival and safe return of their son, Udochukwu after the civil war. The church was packed with local parishioners and invited guests, among whom were some of the biggest names in town, in education, commerce and industry. They included Mr. Azubuike Elendu, General Manager of Golden Breweries; Mr. Johnson Aguomba, Manager of African Continental Bank, Umuahia; Mr. Uchendu Ndubuisi, Principal of Anglican Grammar School, Umuahia; Dr. (Mrs.) Florence Ehiemere, Executive Director of Queen Elizabeth Hospital, Umuahia; Mr. Isaac Ukaegbe, General Manager, Ceramics Industry, Umuahia; Mr. Nelson Nwobodo, Principal of Government College, Umuahia; Dr. Emmanuel Ezeilo, Director-General of Federal School of Agriculture and Roots Research Institute, Umudike; Mr. H.C. Ogbonna, Principal of Oboro Secondary School, Ikwuano; Mr. I.N. Eleazu, Vice Principal of Oboro Secondary School, and C. de Aguomba, Executive Editor of foreign affairs, Renaissance Newspaper, all of whom were invited with their spouses.

After the church service, a lavish reception was held in the sprawling ballroom of Evergreen Hotel in Umuahia town. Udochukwu's parents had spent an enormous amount on the spectacular social treat, which not only featured a broad variety of dishes and drinks, but also live music entertainment by the most popular musicians in the State, *'The Oriental Brothers.'* After the invitees had been served with foods and drinks, it was time for the band to play the music to signal the opening of the dance floor. The Oriental Brothers began with their wildly, popular favorite hit music of the 70s, *"Ebelamu Akw'uwa...."* It was electrifying. The audience broke out in cheers, and guests took to the floor to dance. Udochukwu and his wife, Collette sitting in the front row were visibly thrilled to the core. Albert Abara, Udochukwu's dad with his mother, also sitting in the front row, had sitting next to them, the young woman from their village, whom he'd spoken favorably about as his choice of a potential bride for Udochukwu. The young woman, Ebere had been invited with her parents, Mr. and Mrs. Obike Ukandu as part of the special guests. Halfway into the program after members of the audience had danced to multiple treats of *The Oriental Brothers* music, the master of ceremonies of the occasion introduced the guests of honor, and called upon Udochukwu's father to give a speech. Albert Abara stood up, looked over his shoulder and beckoned the daughter of Mr. and Mrs. Obike Ukandu to come with him to the floor. Surprisingly when Mr. Abara began to speak, his remarks made him sound like a provocateur. He said, "*.... We are grateful to God for saving the life of our son, Udochukwu, and equally thank the white lady who had helped him; nonetheless, I don't think that she is the right one for our son, or merits being his wife. She is too old for him, and besides, she is a foreigner, a white lady for that matter, and not by any means compatible, from a cultural standpoint, our culture to be specific. Alternatively, this fine young woman standing here with me, from our community, is the person we will prefer to be Udochukwu's wife.*"

"Oh, no he didn't!" said someone reacting to the repugnant statement, as some of the guests rolled their eyes in disgust.

An audible gasp was heard from the audience. His unexpected, pernicious remarks about Collette sent chills down her spines, and abruptly changed the exuberant disposition of the audience.

"Jesus Christ! What on earth was that supposed to mean? And having my daughter standing next to him? I can't believe I heard him say that," Mr. Obike Ukandu, the father of the young woman blurted out.

"That wasn't right. He basically used my daughter as a ruse in his speech," Mr. Ukandu plaintively noted with a sigh.

Someone else in the audience was heard saying, "It is so disappointing and shameful of Mr. Albert Abara to say a thing like that. Right now, the story in the village which people are talking about, is how that white lady, the French woman, married to his son, rescued him from the dungeon of captivity in a Nigerian military prison in Calabar after he was captured during the war, and took him to France. The good life he and his family are enjoying now, is attributed to the French woman's generosity. See how many people had come to celebrate with them. It's hard to believe that such an occasion of 'Thanksgiving' with the theme of celebration and gratitude for the compassion and kindness of the human heart, in a stranger from overseas, would be ruined in such a reckless manner. Now people would not remember the event for what it was intended to be — thanksgiving and gratitude — rather they would remember it for the man's ingratitude."

GROANING SOUND WAS HEARD in the ballroom as people began to leave prematurely signaling their disappointment with Udochukwu's father's gratuitous remarks in his speech. Collette, the target of the disparaging comment, was visibly hurt and flustered. She turned to Udochukwu and said to him, "I want to leave now. You have to get me back to the Guest House."

Udochukwu was addled. He and his mother did not seem to show any expression suggesting disapproval of his father's hurtful remarks. It had seemed to Collette like father, mother and son conspiracy, designed to inflict emotional injury and provoke her to terminate the marriage, so they can have the chance to get the young woman from their village, as their preferred choice of a bride for Udochukwu.

Collette got up, and started to leave carrying her child. Udochukwu, looking dejected reluctantly got up and followed behind her. It was the last time Collette would see or talk with Udochukwu's parents.

"Tomorrow Monday, first thing in the morning, please take me to the General Post Office, telecommunications office so that I can make some important phone calls," she told him as they walked to the car to drive back to the Guest House. "I will be traveling back with my child to Federal Palace Hotel in Lagos, for our return flight to France sooner than we'd scheduled. You have the choice to come along with us, or stay behind with your parents; whatever you want to do, it's totally up to you," Collette said in no uncertain terms as soon as they got back to the Guest House.

She knew she was placing Udochukwu in a difficult situation to make the choice, and was well aware of the implicit risk for her, given the strained relations that had developed and how Udochukwu's family at home might react. But at that point, she didn't care and did not want to be dissembling. She wanted to be blunt and candid with Udochukwu about her feelings.

Monday morning, they went to the telecommunications office at the Umuahia General Post Office Building and Collette made the phone calls. One call to the Federal Palace Hotel informing them she was coming back the next day, Tuesday, and requested that her accommodation be reactivated. The other call to the French Embassy in Lagos, notifying them she was coming back to Lagos from her trip to the East, and would be flying back home to France in a few days' time.

"PAPA, WHAT YOU DID YESTERDAY is causing trouble now," Udochukwu told his dad in the presence of his mother, when he drove back to the village. "Now, Collette has decided to return to Lagos, and would be traveling home to France earlier than scheduled," he added.

"Okay, let her go back now, ahn-ahn, what's the big deal? If that's what she wants to do, let her go ahead and leave," said his father tartly, unperturbed. His mother was a little bit nuanced.

"Papa Udochukwu," she addressed him by the pet name she calls him (meaning father of Udochukwu). "I was worried, too about the potential consequence of your unexpected remarks on the white lady, purportedly Udochukwu's wife. As I noted to you earlier, when you had raised the issue regarding your feelings about her and their marriage; it wasn't the right time to express your views or concerns, and certainly not the right place or occasion to do so. It was inappropriate and uncalled for at that setting. Now the whole village will be thinking that we are ingrates."

"By the way, is she leaving with the child?" Udochukwu's mom asked.

"Of course," said Udochukwu. "As things are right now, I have no other choice; I have to leave with her. We're traveling back to Lagos on Tuesday and will subsequently be flying back to France."

"Is that so? What about the important discussion I thought we were going to have concerning your return back home, the transportation business we started that is doing very well, your mother's provisions retail business, the beer and soft drinks distributorship, and your younger brother, Nkem's further education? What would be the fate of these important issues?" asked Udochukwu's father.

"I don't know," Udochukwu shrugged indifferently. "Everything appears to be messed up now and hanging in the balance," he added.

To be more emphatic and put things in perspective, Udochukwu also said, "Papa, remember your job before the war, as *Tracks Maintenance Supervisor* with the Nigerian Railway Corporation at the Umuahia – Port Harcourt Eastern Region rail lines, literally ended at the beginning of the civil war. You were not reinstated after the war, and now you have a thriving private family business in public transportation, trade and commerce with my mom, all thanks to Collette, who was God sent."

His father's response was, "I am not saying the woman is bad, my concern is that she's too old for you and a white woman, which is not culturally compatible and will be a problem."

After Udochukwu and Collette had left with their child back to Lagos for their return trip to France, Albert Abara would have another visitor reminding him of the blunders he committed during his speech at the reception.

"I have come to tell you that what you did at the reception last Sunday during your speech was a disaster," said Mr. Azubuike Elendu, the general manager of Golden Breweries when he made an unannounced visit. "Your views and feelings about your son's wife, the white lady, expressed during your speech at the reception, was uncalled for. In addition, flaunting the younger woman from your village in front of everyone as your preferred choice of a potential bride for your son, was an egregious insult to the white lady who had done incredibly so much for your son. Can you imagine how many people in your village today, wishing they were as lucky as you and your wife were, in having — to use the biblical metaphor — 'manna from heaven,' such a nice, kind white woman, whose compassion and love for your son, literally made your family what it is today? What you did, indeed took ingratitude to a new height. Let me share with you a story about how bad ingratitude is and its potential consequence.

It was back in 1964, in Lagos. An American newspaper in New York City published a story about a man from Aba, who was part of his church group in Nigeria, *'Evangelical Mission of God,'* invited to Michigan for an International Christian Conference sponsored by a church in the United States affiliated with his local church.

Johnson Igwe, 56, was visiting the United States in the summer of 1964. He'd been part of his local church group 'Evangelical Mission of God' in his native town of Aba, Nigeria invited to Detroit, Michigan for a two week International Christian Conference, a summer retreat sponsored by the host church in Michigan affiliated with his local church in Nigeria. The American church had provided supporting documents needed for U.S. travel visa application as proof of financial resources and provision of temporary accommodation for members of the Nigerian church group during their U.S. visit. The U.S. Embassy in Lagos, Nigeria granted each member of the visiting church group 3 months U.S. nonimmigrant Visitors Visa. After the two week conference had ended, Mr. Igwe took advantage of the remaining duration of his 3 months U.S. Visitor Visa to travel to New York City to visit with a kinsman of his from the same village in his home country living in New York. The kinsman in New York had been made aware of Mr. Igwe's visit to Michigan for the International Christian Conference. They'd both communicated by mail ahead of his visit, and the kinsman had agreed that on his way back to Nigeria, he would stop over in New York to visit with him and his family for a few days.

As arranged, Mr. Igwe's kinsman, a naturalized United States Citizen picked him up at New York City Grand Central Terminal, the city's most famous transportation hub where he had arrived on a Greyhound Bus from Detroit, Michigan on a Friday evening. He was well received. The wife of his *kinsman had made a delicious meal considered to be one of their favorite native dishes in honor of their guest. Mr. Igwe was served the native homemade dish with drinks. He ate and drank his fill. On Monday morning, after the host couple had left for work and their three pre-teenage children off to school, Mr. Igwe decided to take a walk around the neighborhood. While in the commercial area of the neighborhood, he'd gone into a retail store to buy a local newspaper and a pack of cigarette. He noticed an advertisement for lottery tickets on the wall behind the counter that said "Win Prize in Mega Millions for One Dollar!" He thought to himself, how about buying a lottery ticket or two? He might as well try his luck, why not? He then bought 2 lottery tickets for the potential Mega Millions prize at a dollar per ticket. He pocketed the tickets and strolled back home to his kinsman's house. Later that night at around 11:30 P.M., while watching the news in the living room after his host family were already asleep, he saw the winning lottery ticket numbers on television when the news anchor made the announcement. He copied the numbers. Alone in the guest bedroom after he'd retreated to go to sleep, he checked the winning numbers against the numbers of the lottery tickets he'd bought earlier in the day. To his wildest surprise, the numbers on one of the tickets he bought corresponded with the winning numbers. And the winning Lottery Jackpot amount: $15.7 MILLION. Mr. Igwe checked the numbers again and again and again. And each time, the numbers he had corresponded with the winning numbers shown on television. He became so overwhelmed, in awe of the* *tremendous fortune he believed would soon be coming his way. So much so that he fell on the floor in the guest bedroom, clutching his chest like someone having a cardiac arrest. After about forty five minutes of laying on the floor, gasping for breath and asking himself, "God, is it me! Is it me! Winner of FIFTEEN MILLION, SEVEN HUNDRED THOUSAND DOLLARS?" he then got up and plopped on the bed. But sleep wouldn't come. He literally stayed up awake all night till the following morning. He decided not to utter one word about the greatest surprise of his life from the day before to his kinsman, when he and his family all got up and were going through the hectic morning routine preparing for daily New York busy life. His kinsman's wife even took the time to make breakfast for him. By the time she left home for work to catch the morning rush-hour subway train to Downtown, Manhattan, New York, traffic congestion had built up. It worsened her commute that Monday morning and caused her to arrive late at work.*

Once everyone had left, leaving Mr. Igwe alone in the house, he turned on the television in the living room to watch the morning news on New York's Channel 7 Eye Witness News, while he sat at the dining table to eat breakfast of fried eggs, bread toast, bacon and cheese with coffee and a glass of orange juice his kinsman's wife had made for him. While he was eating, he saw again a rebroadcast of the winning lottery jackpot ticket numbers he had, and salivated at the prospect of soon-to-become a multimillionaire with $15.7 Million overnight to his name. After having breakfast, he dumped the plates *he ate with in the kitchen sink without even bothering to wash them. He then took a shower, dressed up, and went back to the store where he'd bought the lottery tickets the day before. In the store he recognized the middle-aged Indian looking man with grey-hair and silver beard behind the counter who sold the lottery tickets to him. Half a dozen customers were standing in line waiting to be served. Mr. Igwe went straight to the front of the counter cutting off the customers already in the store standing in line. The store man at the counter politely told him, "Sir, you have to get in line behind the customers and wait for your turn." Some of the customers weren't as polite; they stridently upbraided Mr. Igwe with expletives not uncommon with New Yorkers: "Hey, you ass hole! Get your fucking behind to the back of the line!"*

Mr. Igwe realized he'd made a fool of himself in his eagerness to see about his apparent lottery jackpot win. Embarrassed, he stepped back to the back of the line and waited for his turn.

"Okay, Sir! What can I do for you," the store man behind the counter asked him, when it was his turn to be served.

"I was here yesterday and bought two lottery tickets. It looks like one of the tickets has the winning numbers; could you check for me?"

"Sure," the store man said and fed the tickets into the lottery ticket vending machine one after the other.

"Holy Moses!" his face lit up with an eye-popping expression. "$15.7 MILLION WON. See the store clerk," the lottery vending machine scanner displayed. One of the tickets did indeed show the complete winning numbers in a row with the

whopping sum of $15.7 MILLION. He took the winning ticket from the lottery vending machine and motioned to Mr. Igwe to come with him to the backroom of the store. Inside the backroom, the store man told his wife who was busy taking inventory of merchandise to suspend the activity and go to the counter and attend to customers so he could chat in private with Mr. Igwe. His wife obliged, and he shut the backroom door.

"Hi, I'm Sanjay Gupta, owner of this store," the store man introduced himself, stretching out his hand to Mr. Igwe.

"I'm pleased to meet you," he coyly responded and shook hands with the store man.

"First of all, let me say to you, Congratulations! Do you realize that your life is about to change in a very big way, going forward? You have won the lottery jackpot of $15.7 Million!"

Looking dazed as if day dreaming and trying to process the good news, Mr. Igwe managed to say two words: "Thank you."

"Now tell me," the store man continued—

"I detect you have an accent; do you live in this area, or you're visiting from out of town?"

"I'm visiting from another country as a matter of fact. I came to see my kinsman from my home country who lives here, just for a few days before I travel back home to my country," said Mr. Igwe.

"Oh, I see. You're here on Visitor Visa, or you're a legal Resident Alien with Green Card or U.S. Citizen?"

"Visitor Visa. I'm not a legal Resident or Citizen. My kinsman living here is a U.S. Citizen," Mr. Igwe reeled off candidly.

"Hmmmm," the store man sighed after a brief pause and said: "looks like you're going to have a problem collecting the money because you're not a U.S. Citizen or a legal Resident Alien."

Mr. Igwe's countenance changed dramatically. "How do you mean, I don't understand?" he asked taking a pointed look at the store man.

"I mean, you say you're not a U.S. Citizen or legal Resident Alien. The rule or condition behind the lottery ticket states that you have to be either of the two to collect the lottery jackpot payment."

Mr. Igwe took back the ticket from the store man and verified the rule as stipulated on the reverse side. "What can I do now?" he asked the store man, his voice quivering.

"I'll tell you what you can do."

"The easiest thing you can do, if you want, is to tell your kinsman, your host, about the mega jackpot win, and let him collect the money in his name for you, since he is a U.S. Citizen. You can make a deal, like an agreement to give him a fraction of the amount, say $1 Million or $2 Million or more, whatever amount you both can agree on, in exchange for helping you collect the money. That way it saves you the hassles or complications of a legal hurdle in the attempt to collect the money on your own. The rule clearly doesn't favor you under your current status as a non-legal U.S. Resident Alien or Citizen."

At the store man's suggestion advising Mr. Igwe to inform his kinsman (host) about his lottery jackpot win of $15.7 Million, and make an agreement to have him – being a U.S. Citizen — collect the whopping sum on his behalf in exchange for a fraction of the *money; his face turned sour, like a man who'd just been rescued from a fall into a pit latrine full of human excrement typically found in underdeveloped countries. "Let me think about it," purred, Mr. Igwe. It was clearly visible to the store man that Johnson Igwe was unhappy with the idea of letting his kinsman know about his lottery jackpot win, and involve him in a prudent effort to facilitate the collection of the whooping sum of money.*

"Well, you have plenty of time to think about it, several months at least. So whatever you decide to do, I wish you good luck," said the store man to Mr. Igwe as he walked out of the store looking morose.

He got back to his kinsman's house pondering over his options. Strangely enough, he never mentioned anything about the lottery jackpot winning ticket in his possession to his kinsman and his wife, who'd been very hospitable to him. He was still bent on keeping to himself the good news about the winning lottery jackpot ticket in his possession, and the dilemma surrounding collection of the money. He was hoping he'd somehow figure out a way to collect the staggering amount eventually all by himself. Now on day 5 of his visit with his kinsman and family, he had only a couple of days left for his return flight back to his home country of Nigeria at the expiration of his Visitor Visa. He would depart from New York's JFK International Airport as scheduled the coming Friday at noon. In their spirit of hospitality, his kinsman took him to the airport and saw him off when it was time to board the plane for departure.

Two days after he arrived Nigeria, Johnson Igwe went to the American Embassy in Lagos quixotically thinking he could solicit the assistance of the embassy to collect the lottery jackpot win. Sadly, he learned there was no such assistance the embassy could render to him. 'Sorry, that was a situation you could and should have taken care of while you were still visiting the U.S. under the legal sponsorship of your hosts,' a U.S. Consular Officer told him, when he brought out the winning ticket and showed the embassy official."

"That was how Johnson Igwe deprived himself of the $15.7 Million he won with the purchase of 2 lottery tickets for two dollars during his visit to America," noted Mr. Elendu. "The story had it that when he finally returned home to Aba, his wife noticed he was looking sad on arrival, as if something bad had happened to him. He reportedly told his wife the story of his lottery jackpot win while visiting with his kinsman in New York, and the stupid mistake he made in not letting him know about it. His kinsman, who was a naturalized American Citizen, he was advised, was his best possible realistic option to collect the whooping sum, since he could not, by reason of law, collect the money being a non-Legal Resident Alien or Citizen of the United States. He showed his wife the winning lottery ticket validated with the prize amount the store man had printed out for him. His wife grimaced in pain, and for the first time in their marriage, scornfully heaped a tirade of insults on him: *'ibu Ewu! Uburu Nama ka nke gi nma!'* (Meaning in their native vernacular, 'you are a goat!' Cow's brain is better than yours.')"

"What the hell are you showing me the lottery ticket for, hah?" she was said to have fumed and asked him. "The show of ingratitude in your behavior toward your son's wife, the French woman as manifested by your remark at the reception party, is similar to the ingratitude as depicted in the U.S. newspaper story about   Mr. Igwe, the Aba man who went on a church conference to America. If not for Mr. Igwe's ingratitude, he'd have easily collected through his kinsman, a U.S. Citizen, the millions of dollars in lottery jackpot he won during his U.S. visit. It wasn't too long after that his visit that the ethnic conflicts in Nigeria resulted in the civil war. Had he collected the huge sum of money from the lottery jackpot payout through his kinsman in New York, he probably would have been advised to open a bank account in New York and deposit a substantial part of it in the account, or done some other forms of financial investments, say, in stocks, bonds or what have you. Over the three year span of the civil war, he'd have had huge sums of money waiting for him in the U.S. in bank accounts or other investment portfolios after the civil war. But greed and ingratitude occluded his sense of reason, and his foolishness cost him a fortune of a lifetime. Because there was no legitimate claimant that came along, the money ended up somewhere else. The old proverb says that 'One good turn deserves another.' I have the feeling you might have vitiated any future chances of that French woman's benevolence, and what that would mean for your son going forward," said Mr. Azubuike Elendu, the general manager of Golden Breweries.

Udochukwu affirmed his decision to return to Lagos with his wife and child.

"Does that mean traveling back to France with us, too?" Collette asked him.

"Yes," he said.

TUESDAY MORNING. With their luggage packed and ready to go, the driver of the 504 Peugeot, who'd been chauffeuring them about during their visit, drove them to Enugu Airport accompanied by Udochukwu's younger brother, Nkem. They left Umuahia around 8:00 A.M. Nigeria Airways operated local daily flights from Enugu to Lagos. They would go with the late afternoon flight leaving at 4:30 P.M. Collette bought their tickets for First Class seats when they arrived the airport much earlier. They went into the airport's VIP Lounge to stay since they had some time to kill before departure. About thirty minutes before boarding, a middle-aged man with a mixture of grey, white and dark beard walked into the VIP Lounge surrounded by some civilian aides and two armed soldiers as his personal security detail. He saw Collette sitting in a three-seater couch with Udochukwu and their child in between them, and made eye contacts.

"Hello, Madam," the man said, and shook hands with Collette and Udochukwu.

"I am Ukpabi Asika, the Administrator of East Central State. Welcome to our part of the world," he said to Collette in a preening effort to look congenial toward her and her husband. "Is this your husband?" he asked.

"*Oui*, Yes," said Collette.

"I detect an accent, possibly French?" he guessed.

"Yes, yes," said Collette.

"Oh, that's nice, pleased to meet both of you," said Mr. Asika.

Until that brief exchange of pleasantries with the States' most prominent high profile figure, there had been very little interaction between Collette and Udochukwu. While Collette focused her attention on her son playfully mimicking baby talk with him in a deliberate effort to avoid communication with Udochukwu, he on the other hand, remained muted.

At 4:30 P.M., the Nigeria Airways local flight to Lagos rumbled off the runway en route to Ikeja, Lagos Airport. They landed in Lagos roughly forty five minutes later, and caught a cab to Federal Palace Hotel. Collette's icy behavior had continued throughout the flight from Enugu to Lagos. It was no different from what it was in the cab ride from Ikeja airport to the Federal Palace Hotel. After breakfast Wednesday morning, Collette called the booking office of Air France on Broad Street, near Tinubu Square, to change the date of their return flight to France.

"It would cost you extra fee to make the change," said the Air France ticketing agent on the phone.

"That's okay," Collette downplayed the extra fee. All that mattered to her was getting the earliest possible flight out of Lagos to Paris. The earliest date available was for a flight leaving on Friday the same week.

The rift had been incredibly challenging for Udochukwu and Collette. Reflecting on the mind numbing experience she had at Udochukwu's hometown, Collette could not bring herself to having any normal, cordial communication with him just yet.

The emotional wound inflicted by Udochukwu's father in his repugnant remark on Collette during his speech at the reception, was still fresh on her mind. Once they boarded the plane and took their seats, she turned to Udochukwu and looked him in the eye and said, "Now I know that no matter where, human beings are all the same. But it is totally up to the individual, for whatever the reason, to choose to bend or not to bend, to the dictates of human prejudices."

During the flight back to France, there was hardly any interaction between the two of them as a couple. She was still brooding sentimentally over the remarks. The sheer temerity of Udochukwu's father disparagingly commenting that she was too old for his son, and flaunting in her face, a younger woman from his home village, whom he said their family preferred to be Udochukwu's wife, sounded so brutal and terribly hard to repress. A deluge of memories flooded her mind. She recalled the things she went out of her way and did for Udochukwu, which included, risking her life and freedom, career and reputation, in a surreptitious plot she conceived and executed in sneaking Udochukwu out of the dungeon of captivity in a military prison in Calabar, Nigeria and brought him to France. In addition, defying the attendant negative implications of her interracial marriage because she unapologetically loved Udochukwu, not to talk of how his parents had benefited immensely from her unconditional love for their son. Looking downcast, against the backdrop of all of those things she'd done for Udochukwu purely out of love and compassion, she winced in pain and bit her lip in regrets, then turned her face away from him.

After the flight landed in Paris and they disembarked the plane; what happened next from then on? — The riveting Sequel.

About the Author

Educated at Oboro Secondary School (formerly Oboro Methodist Grammar School), Oboro, Ikwuano Local Government Area, Abia State, Nigeria; Ukachi Uwadinobi went to America for higher education. He is a graduate of San Diego State University, San Diego, California. He holds associate degrees in Liberal Arts and Science, a bachelor's degree in Economics, and a master's degree in Business Administration (MBA). After a long and successful career in hospital quality management in New York, he retired in 2023.